# HAY

---

## A MADE MARIAN SHORT

## LUCY LENNOX

*Thank you:*

*Sloane, Shay, Chad, and Victoria for invaluable beta feedback.*

*Molly for telling me it needed work after I said it needed work. (Sisters, I swear to dog.)*

*Cate for nailing the cover.*

*Sandra for editing with flair.*

# HAY

When sports journalist Hayworth Buchanan lands the interview of
his dreams, he gets the chance to visit famous NFL coach Christian
Lasley at his secluded ranch in Wyoming. Despite the cold weather
outside, things get plenty steamy inside when sparks fly between Hay
and his celebrity sports crush. But Hay's been down this road before,
and he knows from experience hot connections never turn into the
real deal for him. After all, everyone he's ever been interested in has
left him for their childhood love.

So when Christian's on-again, off-again childhood love shows up at
the ranch hoping to reconcile, Hayworth knows he a decision to
make. Does he hand over the ball and slink off the field, or does he
step up and try to make the winning play?

*Hay is a 25k word short story and though it is set in the Made Marian
world, it stands completely on its own.*

# AUTHOR'S NOTE

I've taken artistic license in creating a fictional NFL team located in Jackson, WY. While I'm clear on the impracticalities of such a team, I didn't want one of my main characters to steal an existing coach's job, nor did I want to have to get every detail of a real team's roster, records, and facilities correct.

So, thank you to reader Kaitlin Durante who supplied me with the name Jackson Jackals. Thank you also to reader Marcine Jenck for suggesting the Oregon Pioneers whom I used in several older versions of the story despite not including them in the final. They were just plain too tired after their long journey, so really... who could blame them?

Finally, thank you to reader Mariah Lasley for having a lovely surname.

If you'd like to contribute to future Lucy Lennox stories, please join the fun at https://www.facebook.com/groups/lucyslair/ where readers make suggestions, authors give away prizes, and I reveal the inner-workings of a slightly crazy, noticeably forgetful, often potty-mouthed author.

# 1

## HAYWORTH

I REMEMBER where I was the first time I saw Christian Lasley in person. My high school football team had put on a fund-raiser in which one of the raffle prizes was a pair of tickets to an Atlanta Falcons football game. My dad had bid an insane amount of money to win those tickets so the two of us could go see the Falcons beat the Broncos.

That didn't happen.

Instead, thanks in part to the incredible talents of Denver's new wide receiver, Christian Lasley, Denver crushed the Falcons in a display that my father called thereafter "Falcons Roadkill Day." But that wasn't what I called it. I called it "the day I could no longer deny I was gay."

Because when that wide receiver came off the field in a triumphant strut of glory, he whipped off his helmet, revealing the most beautiful chiseled face I'd ever seen under a head full of wavy blond hair. He'd looked like one of my sister Bailey's Ken dolls come to life. His uniform was making love to his perfect fucking body, and sweat shimmered on his golden skin. I remember snorting and thinking, *Is this guy for real?*

Yes. Yes, he was for real. And he was fan-fucking-tastic.

I'd gone back to Charleston and immediately found my friend-with-benefits Beau Talmadge and thrown him down on the nearest surface, which happened to have been the bed of my pickup truck, and sucked his cock like it was the first time I'd discovered sweet tea.

Unfortunately, my joy at being attracted to the same sex hadn't lasted. That Sunday I'd been reminded in the pulpit why good boys didn't make bad "lifestyle choices." It had taken me ten more years and a shit-ton of pain before finally doing away with the pulpit crap.

And now here I was about to meet Christian Lasley for an interview.

After five years of busting my ass to build a popular sports comedy blog, I'd finally found my calling when I'd turned it into a podcast. Each week I riffed on the most entertaining stories in sports and the funniest plays from that week's games. Several of my episodes had gone viral over the past year, and my subscriptions numbers were through the roof. Apparently, I had fans I didn't even know about, including one Christian Lasley, former Heisman trophy winner, Super Bowl winner, and current coach of the Jackson Jackals. And the man who had recently shocked the sports world by announcing he was gay.

Trying to navigate a giant rental SUV down the snowy gravel drive in rural Wyoming reminded me I was from South Carolina. I didn't know beans about navigating a vehicle in the snow. I could only hope the slow pace I was going was a good thing instead of a mistake. With each jaw-rattling pass over metal bars set into the farm road, I cursed my ignorance of all things... *ranch*.

I was more of a country club boy than a cowboy. The closest I ever got to ranching was when a crudité platter had tasteless carrots on it and needed to be dredged through some dip. I may have ridden a horse once in a video game, but even that was a suspect memory.

As I drove past a fenced pasture, I saw several horses running through the snow in the distance. It was a beautiful sight, like something from a movie. The road curved around until several buildings came into view. One dark red barn with its big doors wide open had several men in cowboy costumes loading items into the bed of a beat-up pickup truck. Well, I guessed they weren't costumes so much as... whatever cowboys who worked on ranches wore on a regular day.

Suffice to say the tight jeans and broken-in boots looked delish from where I sat, and when I spotted two of the men with leather chaps over their jeans, I almost salivated.

Hm, I had a cowboy fetish. Who knew?

But then again, I had a *man* fetish, plain and simple. Once I'd finally faced my true sexuality head-on in my late twenties, well, let's just say I'd moved to San Francisco to make up for lost time.

And make up, I did. I'd done more than my share of clubbing and Grindr-ing, but lately I seemed to be feeling my age more. The casual hookup wasn't cutting it anymore, but if there was one thing I'd learned from the men I'd dated in the past, it was that I wasn't long-term material. I was fun-for-now material. Which was getting old.

Having said that, if one of those cowboys wanted to take me for a ride while I was in town overnight... well, I wouldn't say no.

One of the men waved his hand for me to park on the far side of the barn away from the loading. When I got out and hopped down from the SUV, an older weather-beaten man walked up pulling off a leather glove.

"Perry Jones, ranch foreman. You must be here for Coach."

I nodded. "Hayworth Buchanan. He around?"

The man gestured toward what appeared to be the main residence on the property down a long shoveled path through the snow. The large one-and-a-half-story farmhouse was wide and solid, with deep covered porches across the entire width of the front and a row of dormer windows across the roofline. A thick layer of snow bordered the edges of the house, and I wondered if it covered shrubs that would normally appear in summer.

"Thanks," I said before turning to head toward the house.

"Go easy," the foreman said under his breath. I wasn't quite sure what he meant, but if he'd been referring to the interview itself, there was no chance I was going easy on Christian Lasley. For whatever reason, I'd been lucky enough to land the only sit-down with him the

League had granted, and I wasn't about to fuck it up by being a door-mat. It was a once-in-a-lifetime opportunity for someone like me.

Before I had a chance to knock on the front door, the man himself opened it.

And all thoughts of the other cowboys disappeared in a puff of smoke.

Coach Lasley was, of course, even sexier in person than he appeared on television or even in my memories. The man was a walking wet dream, and if I'd been out in school, I might have even had his damned poster on my bedroom wall. He was that hot. And tall as all hell. He had to be at least three or four inches over six feet. In his late thirties, his hair was still thick and golden, and he even had a chin dimple like a movie star. I wondered idly if his teeth gleamed when he smiled.

"Unf," I grunted.

He tilted his head and furrowed his brow. Of course, it only made him look more stunning. "Are you Mr. Buchanan?"

"Ngh."

This wasn't happening. No fucking way was I losing my cool in front of this legend. I coughed and made a big production out of making it look like there was something in my throat before finally reaching out to shake his hand.

"Sorry, I think my saliva froze."

*Smooth, Hay. Real smooth.*

He laughed, which punched in the famous dimple on his cheek and brightened his eyes. "It's only thirty degrees outside. Wait till the temperature drops in a few hours. Where the hell are you from?"

"South Carolina," I said. "Charleston. Well, I live in the Bay Area now, but I was born and raised in the South."

His smile widened as he stepped back to let me in. "I knew it. Could tell by your accent. Southern boy. Come on in and let's get you warmed up. You prefer coffee or tea?"

I took a step into the house and noticed the polished wood floors. Coach Lasley was wearing socks with no shoes. There was a tray next to the front door with a tumble of different boots and shoes in it. I kicked my own off and tossed them in the tray before following him farther into the house.

"It's a beautiful house. Didn't you grow up here?"

"I did. My parents retired from ranching a few years ago and moved to Florida. I bought them out so I could keep the place. I've always loved it here, and when I committed to the Jackals, I took it as a sign I was meant to stay."

"How have you managed running the place when you have such a demanding job with the team?"

"Our foreman has been with us for over twenty years. He could run the place in his sleep. And it's not such a big operation that I'm not able to help during the off-season when I want."

I thought about him leaving the team headquarters after a long day of meetings and practice and driving to a secluded ranch in the rural outskirts of a small town. He'd never appeared to date anyone in public, but that made sense now. Had there ever been someone waiting for him at home? Living on a ranch would give him a ton of privacy. He could have a love life the public simply didn't know about.

"Hayworth?"

I blinked up at him. Coach Lasley stood at the counter with his hand on the top of a Keurig coffee maker. He'd obviously asked me something. "Sorry, I was just... um..."

"Why don't you pick out the one you want. That might be easier," he said with a kind smile, pushing a basket of various K-Cups over to me. I rooted through the basket until I found a hazelnut blend and handed it to him.

"Thanks. This is a beautiful house," I said before realizing I had become a broken record. "Dammit, sorry. I'm..." I let out a laugh. "I'm a little nervous; not gonna lie."

As he put the K-Cup into the machine and hit the button to start it, he glanced over at me. The blue plaid button-down shirt he wore set off the color variations in his eyes. Years of squinting into the sun had imprinted fine lines beside his eyes that crinkled when he smiled.

"No reason to be."

"You're Christian Lasley," I said. "You were the number two draft pick the day I got my driver's license in high school. When I started blogging, your promotion to head coach was some of the most exciting news to hit the NFL in years. Hell, your first year starting for the Huskers was their first undefeated season in forever. You caught that ball against Iowa with one damned finger."

I realized he was laughing at me. "Is that right? I didn't know any of that stuff. You must have one of them internet doohickies."

Heat flooded my face. "Sorry, it's pretty surreal for me right now. I'm just a random blogger. I'm nobody."

Coach's smile dropped. "Not true. Your show is the hottest thing out there these days."

I realized how fanboy and unprofessional I sounded and finally tried to get my shit together. I didn't want him to regret picking me.

"Thank you. I've worked hard at it for six years. I'm proud of the work I've done, and I appreciate this opportunity."

He studied me for a minute before going back to the task of making my coffee. Once he had cups for each of us, he handed them to me and grabbed a little carton of cream and bowl of sugar. "Let's sit at the table where the cookies are. Now that the season is underway, I'm working off enough calories to justify it," he said with a laugh. "Those guys are giving me a run for my money, especially the receivers. They seem to enjoy making me put my money where my mouth is."

"If I had you as a receiving coach, I'd do the same," I admitted with a laugh. "They want to see you work your magic."

I followed him to a solid wood farmhouse table next to large glass windows. The view from the back of the house was like something from a museum poster.

"This is incredible," I said. "Are those the skiing mountains in Jackson?"

He followed my gaze. "Yeah. Jackson Hole. Those are the Tetons. Never gets old. Gorgeous, isn't it? Wait till you see it at sunset."

"Are you sure you don't mind me staying? I could always get a hotel or someth—"

Coach Lasley interrupted me with a raised hand and a smile. I swear my crush on the man got bigger in that moment. If it was possible. "It's no problem at all. I'm used to it since the ranch is so far out of town, and honestly, I'll feel better if you stay here. If you tried driving these icy roads at night and got into trouble, you'd freeze to death."

I laughed. "I do have a cell phone."

He shook his head and took a sip of his coffee before responding. "Shitty reception on the highway till you get close to town. Doesn't matter anyway. I have plenty of room. Plus, the hotel won't have a replay of the 49ers game you missed while you were in the air."

His dimpled grin shot fireworks off in my stomach. I was going to watch a professional football game with Coach Christian Fucking Lasley? Surely, I was dreaming.

We drank our coffee, chatting about the Bengals' loss to the Bears on Thursday night. Hearing his insight into the Cincinnati defense was eye-opening, and when he explained the way he'd coach the Bears' wide receivers differently, I was fascinated. The conversation must have lasted much longer than I thought, because before I knew it, he was pointing out the window at the most amazing sunset.

"It's like a rainbow," I said, in awe of the warm pinks and oranges and violets. "It's gorgeous."

"That reminds me of why you're here. I didn't mean to go on and on about football."

I chuckled. "Coach, hearing you go on and on about football is a dream for someone like me. I've been in love with the game since I turned four and Santa brought me an orange and blue Nerf football."

"Please call me Christian or Chris."

Nerves coiled in my gut as I tried not to say something stupid again.

"And you can call me Hayworth or Hay. I guess we should get started with the interview, then. Where would you like to do this?"

# 2

## CHRISTIAN

My god, the man was beautiful. I'd been a fan of his blog and podcast for a while now, but had never seen a photo of him or watched any of his YouTube videos. And that was probably a good thing. Because after just one look, I was hooked. As in, wanna eat him for breakfast and then turn right around and do it again for lunch, hooked.

As I led him into the small den off the kitchen, I gestured for him to take one of the two overstuffed chairs in front of the stone fireplace while I started the fire. I could have said I'd chosen the smaller room because it was more comfortable, more intimate, for a conversation, but I was shallower than that. I'd chosen it because in this room, I could sit right across from him in this closely set pair of chairs and look at his sparkling eyes. I could study the angle of his jaw and the neatly styled dark hair. His fuller bottom lip and the wide set of his muscular shoulders. The fact Hayworth Buchanan hadn't gotten his own sports television show yet—if for no other reason than his good looks—was a travesty. Add to that his extensive knowledge of the game and his ability to entertain while summarizing the week's games, players, and news, and I couldn't believe he hadn't been snatched up by one of the networks.

After starting the fire, I sat in the chair across from Hayworth. He'd pulled out a slim laptop and connected some kind of small electrical box to it with a USB cable before attaching two wired lapel microphones to it.

"That's quite a setup," I said. "It looks like you do this kind of thing often."

He looked up with a smile. "Yeah. More and more. At first it was just me in my apartment talking into a void. But now that my reach is growing, I'm doing more traveling and in-person interviews. It's pretty cool. I got to go to the combine last year and interview some of the top college players before the draft. I still have my press badge hanging by my desk."

I thought about how many combines I'd been to. How long had it been since I'd felt that sense of awe? I remembered it. The jagged nerves in my stomach when I'd arrived there as a player. The shell-shock of running into famous coaches and some of the college players I'd admired from afar or on the field. The pressure of performing my best in all the physical challenges so I'd be rated high in the draft. Seeing Hay's face light up talking about it brought some of that excitement back.

"Who'd you interview? Anyone interesting?"

He continued to set up his equipment as he spoke. "Yeah. Garvey Jones. Tonio Cooper. I even sat down with Rishad Sims. Man, that kid can catch a ball. Did you see him in that game against—"

"Cleveland? Where he jumped over Hunt and... what was that guy's name? The DB?"

Hayworth looked up, eyes shining. "Samuelson. Yeah. That shit was insane. Here. It's a lavalier mic. You can run the cord behind you and bring it around your collar. That way it isn't trying to pull itself off your shirt the whole time."

He was adorable if he thought I didn't know how to handle a lavalier mic. "Got it," I said with a wink, taking it from his hand. I noticed his cheeks pinken as he sat back to put his own mic on.

When I took my phone out of my pocket to silence it before the interview, I saw a missed text from Perry telling me he and the ranch hands had left a couple of hours earlier to head to Idaho Falls for the night to take advantage of me being home on a Sunday night during our bye week. Which reminded me I needed to keep an eye on our mare while they were gone.

"Remind me when we're done to go check on a horse," I said, silencing the phone and sticking it back in my pocket. "She's pregnant and everyone else is gone."

"Really? I'd love to come with you, if you don't mind. I've never seen a horse up close. Well, besides the carriage horses in Charleston, but I try to avoid the tourist areas."

My jaw dropped. "Seriously? You've never ridden a horse?"

"Don't tease me now. I'm a beach bum. We don't have horses at the beach."

"Not true. What about the wild ponies in the Outer Banks? Or Cumberland Island?"

Hay was so damned cute when he grinned. "Those are in North Carolina and Georgia respectively. I'm from Charleston. We have rats, squirrels, and bats. You should come visit. It's a hoot."

I snorted. "Uh, no thanks. Wait. Don't you have those painted lady houses too?"

He threw his head back in a real laugh, and for a split-second thought I wished he'd already been recording.

"No, that's San Francisco, where I live now. The colorful houses in Charleston are called Rainbow Row. And before you say it, yes, I agree it should be the other way around. I mean, c'mon. Rainbow? San Fran? And painted ladies are much more Southern than Californian."

"Why'd you move to California?" I asked.

He looked up again and met my eyes for a beat before his mouth widened into a flirty grin. "Long story. The short version is, you, Michael Sam, and I have a history of playing for the same team," he said, referring to the only openly gay man to be drafted by the NFL.

I snorted, appreciating the confirmation he was gay. He was out on his show, but seeing him admit it in person still put me at ease. "The Rams? You ought to be ashamed of yourself."

Hayworth's smile widened and his cheeks flushed. He was goddamned adorable. "Why me? The League's media coordinator said you requested me specifically."

"I'm a fan of your show, and I thought it made the most sense to give the interview to a gay reporter. I hope you don't mind me saying that, but I felt more comfortable talking to someone I knew would understand. Not only are you gay, but you're an athlete and a football lover. You're pretty much the perfect man for me."

# 3

## HAYWORTH

I was pretty sure my brain exploded. And that was saying a lot since I'd already seen his Heisman trophy on the shelf in the study and had managed to remain calm.

Until he said he liked my show and I was the perfect man for him. "Um, what?"

Christian's grin was like something out of a fashion magazine. Chiseled and perfect. It was making me stupid. And hearing-impaired.

"I'm sorry. I'm being inappropriate. I knew you had a sexy voice, but I wasn't prepared for you to also be handsome as hell in person."

I tilted my head at him, trying to determine if he was flirting or putting me on. "Are you..." I wheezed. "You're..."

"Do you need me to slap your face like in the movies?"

"You. Christian Lasley. Think I'm handsome."

This was me being professional. Apparently.

"Those are the facts as I've relayed them here today," Christian said, imitating a television attorney. "This can't be the first you're hearing of your attractiveness."

I held up a finger. "Gimme a second."

My brain whirred through a million different thoughts. What it meant if Christian Lasley was both gay and attracted to me. What it meant if I had a chance at a hookup with a football giant.

Christian chuckled. "Take your time. It's not like I have anything else better to do. Cough, 49ers game, cough."

I couldn't help but snort out a laugh. Who knew the man had a funny bone?

"Pfft, you already told me it's recorded. You have to admit, this is a big deal," I confessed, meaning landing the only interview with him about his sexuality.

He nodded. "Yes. It's been a while since I was this attracted to someone."

I felt my face heat, shocked to the core at his flirty behavior I'd seen absolutely no hint of in the media. "Are you for real? What happened to Coach Stoic-Pants?"

"Is that what they call me behind my back? Don't you think we can come up with something better? It makes me sound like I'm related to SpongeBob."

"Have you always been so flirty?"

"Definitely not. I was way too scared. But that's why I came out. I'm ready to have a life."

"What do you mean?"

"I dated a guy on and off for many years. Keeping it secret was miserable. When we broke up the final time, I suddenly got enough distance to see how toxic all that secrecy was. I don't want to do that anymore."

"I assume the decision was hard as hell."

"Definitely. I love this game, and I want it all. Football, a love life... I don't think it's fair for them to be mutually exclusive."

"I agree. I thought it was so exciting when Matt Pacifici introduced his partner on Instagram like it was no big deal. I can't wait till more and more players feel that free. That's why I'm out on my show."

"That's one of the reasons I picked you. I admire you for the way you handle it. And obviously, I just love the show itself... your style."

I looked up in surprise from where I'd been fiddling with my computer. "Really?"

"On your show you treat football like it's fun. So many of the networks act like it's big business or it's a serious matter to be analyzed like a lab experiment. And they're not wrong. It's just... it's nice to see someone remind us of the fun side. And your podcast does that. You also show the heart in the game. When players have heartbreaking misses or triumphant personal victories. I love that."

My face heated under his praise. "Thank you," I murmured. "I... wow. That's the nicest thing anyone's ever said about it."

We locked eyes for a moment before he shrugged and looked away. "What can I say? I'm a nice guy."

His discomfort was kind of cute. It was very different from his usual commanding manner on the football field.

"I guess you are," I said with a smile. "On that note, let's get started."

After a detailed intro about him, I went right into the topic of his coming out. He explained how he approached his team management and then League management before making the decision to come out during a preseason press conference. Their hopes had been to get the word out early so that by the time the season got underway, media attention would have died down.

"And has it?" I asked.

Christian barked out a laugh. "You're here, aren't you?"

"Touché," I said with a wink.

# 4

## CHRISTIAN

The interview was straightforward, and we got through the first half of it—the part about my sexuality—before deciding to take a break to check on the pregnant mare.

After setting his equipment down on the small table between the two chairs, Hayworth stood and followed me back through the kitchen to the front hall where our boots and coats were. I noticed his preppy cotton button-down shirt tucked into khaki pants. He didn't have on anything warmer besides the coat he'd come in.

"Is that all you have to wear besides your coat?" I asked. "No fleece or sweater or anything?"

He looked down at himself as if he'd forgotten what he had on. "Um, I have a sweatshirt in my bag in the car."

I shook my head. "It'll already be freezing. Let me grab you something from upstairs. Wait here."

After running up the steps to my bedroom, I fished out the thickest hoodie I could find and a pair of wool socks. There were extra beanies and gloves in a box in the barn. I returned to the front hall and handed the hoodie to Hayworth.

Hay's eyes widened. "Oh my god. You're so never getting this back. Is this yours?"

I looked at the bright red Nebraska Football sweatshirt. There were probably fifteen similar pullovers in my big closet upstairs, along with all kinds of gear and merchandise from other teams I'd been part of or even played against. I shrugged. "Yeah. You can keep it. No worries. I have a million of them."

He pulled it over his head and hugged himself around the middle melodramatically. "I'm wearing an actual, *vintage* Christian Lasley Huskers hoodie. Holy crap. I'm totally auctioning this online when I get home. Gonna buy myself a penthouse in downtown San Francisco with the profits."

I clapped him on the shoulder. "Enough with the 'vintage' comments. If you were in high school when I was drafted, that means you're only five or six years younger than I am."

He shot me a cheeky grin. "Six. And I'll *always* be six years younger than you."

"Smart-ass," I muttered, pulling on my coat and handing him his.

We made our way down the path toward the barn, walking over new snow that had begun to fall just in the time it had taken to record the first part of the interview. Gone were the colorful streaks in the sky, and in their place were the cold steel-gray clouds of a snowstorm.

"Did you make it here okay in the snow?" I asked, keeping a close eye on Hayworth's footing as we walked through the shadowy path. There were exterior lights along the walkway as well as the flood-lights on the barn up ahead, but it was still next to impossible to discern what was solid ground and what was ice.

"Since when does it snow in September?" he asked.

"Since this is Wyoming," I teased.

Hayworth turned to say something else over his shoulder at me and nearly wiped out on a slick spot. I grabbed his elbow to keep him from face-planting in the snowbank.

"Easy, greenhorn. You're not in Kansas anymore," I warned with a chuckle.

Hayworth clasped my hand after I threaded my arm through his. His grip was warm and strong. "Shit. That damned near gave me a heart attack. Here and I thought I only had to worry about making a fool of myself during the interview."

"Nah. Here at the Flying L Ranch, we give you all kinds of opportunities to make a fool of yourself. Just wait till you have to assist me in castrating a bull."

Hay gasped and slipped again. I wasn't sure if his surprise was at my joke or from actually slipping.

When we finally got to an area with more scattered hay and gravel, it was easier to keep our footing. I reluctantly let go of him and walked ahead to open the barn door. My dog, Brownie, greeted me enthusiastically, followed by a more mellow greeting from the pair of Great Pyrenees who lived in the barn.

Hayworth squatted down to give them some attention.

"It's heated in here, but not well enough to take off any of your gear," I told him. "Come here and let me find you some gloves and a hat. We have insulated coveralls if you get too cold in what you're wearing."

"How long do you expect us to be out here?" he asked.

"As long as it takes." I found a wool beanie and shoved it on Hayworth's head, taking great pride in fucking with his perfectly styled hair.

"Oiy!" he cried, trying to pull it off. We wrestled over it until we both seemed to realize our faces were only inches from each other. The white puffs of our breaths hovered between us as our eyes met.

"You are a handsome man, Hayworth Buchanan," I murmured.

"And you have a dimple on your chin like Aaron Eckhart, Christian Lasley," he said softly.

"Who?"

"That actor... what was he in? The one with the chin dimple."

I grinned at him, and Hay's lips widened in a sexy smile.

He stepped closer until my knees brushed his thighs and then said, "Sully. He was the copilot. Aaron Eckhart was."

"The guy with the big fat mustache?" I asked

Hayworth nodded. "Uh-huh."

I could feel the warm air from his exhales against the skin of my neck.

"But I don't have a mustache," I breathed. I wanted to kiss him so badly, I could hardly think of anything else. I knew it was wrong, but I couldn't seem to stop myself. I leaned in.

"No you don't..." he said. "Let me check to be sure?"

After only the slightest answering lean from him, I moved the rest of the way and brushed my lips across his before taking his lower lip between mine.

It was so soft and plump. I grazed it with my teeth until his breath caught.

"We shouldn't do this," he said in a whisper. "I'm a journalist and... you're..."

"I know."

I deepened the kiss and wrapped my hands around his waist. We were both wearing such bulky clothing, there wasn't much to feel, but the taste of him was incredible and I wanted to savor it for hours.

"Fuck you taste good," Hayworth said between kisses. "I should have picked the kind of coffee you did."

I pulled back enough to cup his face. "You can stop me if you want. You know that, right?"

"And these horses probably have glittery wings and can fly."

His cheeks were pink from the cold, and his eyes shone in the shadowy barn. He was so handsome and engaging. Now that I had him here, I didn't want to ever let him go.

"I guess we should check on our pregnant mare before the snow gets too deep. We wouldn't want to have to spend the night in here with the animals."

Hayworth looked around. "I don't know. Seems okay. Lots of... *hay*."

"I've always liked... *hay*."

He chuckled and pushed me farther along toward the horse stalls. "Then quit stalling so you can go back to getting some."

**5**

---

## HAYWORTH

MY LIPS WERE tingling and my entire body buzzing after kissing Christian. All I could think about while he led me down the aisle between the stalls was what my teenage self would say if he could see me now. It was like a fantasy come to life.

"I didn't come out until I was twenty-eight," I blurted at the back of his head. I wasn't sure why I wanted him to know we had a little something in common, but I did.

He turned back to me. "Really? Why not?"

When I caught up with him, he was opening the door to an extra-large stall at the end of the barn. I could see a dark brown horse with an even darker brown mane. She wasn't quite as big and scary as I'd been expecting. Until, of course, she made some kind of horsey *pfft* noise that scared the pants off me.

"Jesus fuck," I squeaked, jumping back.

"Her name is Dottie."

"Surely not." She looked far too stately to be given such a Midwestern church lady's name.

"Come here and let me show you."

He walked into the stall, murmuring endearments to her while petting her long nose. I followed behind him, using Christian's body as my very own human shield. When we got closer to her hind end, I noticed the huge bulge of her belly.

"She's pregnant!"

He chuckled. "I told you that already."

"I know, but look how fat she is."

The smooth brown fur over her rounded belly shifted, and I grabbed on to Christian's shoulder in surprise.

"Holy shit! There's something in there."

"A colt. Hopefully. Or a filly would be fine too. We're a little mare-heavy right now though. Look here."

I looked at where he pointed to the top of her hip and saw a small spray of black dots focused in an area about the size of my palm.

"Dottie," I said.

"Yep."

As the horse shifted her weight, I had mental images of being crushed up against the wall of her stall.

"I'm... yeah. I'm gonna just step back out into the hallway here," I said, scooting back toward the stall door. "And, uh, let you do... whatever it is you do to pregnant horses."

"Don't tell me you're chickenshit. You played defensive back against those giants from Conway."

I froze in my tracks and stared at him. His smirk told me he knew exactly how off guard he'd caught me.

"You're not the only one who did his research before today's interview, Hayworth."

"That... that game was a fluke. I usually played offense like you," I said stupidly, like it mattered. "I got my ass kicked that night."

"You helped keep that team to two field goals."

We'd been so fucking proud of ourselves that night. I remembered the team captain, Nate Clowder, slapping my butt after that game with his big meaty hand and telling me what a great job I'd done. Man, what I wouldn't have given to have him do other things to me that night with those hands. The man had been over six feet of muscle and sweat.

"That's why not," I said. "Why I didn't come out. Same reasons as you. Even though I only played through college, it was still a big fucking deal. And after that... well. I still lived in a small Southern town. My parents are friends with everyone, and I was terrified of rocking the boat."

Christian nodded. "I get it. I definitely get it. I'm thirty-eight years old, and I'm still nervous about upsetting my parents."

"Do they know?"

"Oh yeah. They know all right. And they would have done just about anything to keep the lid turned tight on that one. Forever if possible. If I insisted on being gay, I could at least have the decency to marry a quiet local man who would keep it on the down low."

"The guy you mentioned before?"

I noticed Christian smoothing his hands over the horse's big belly while he leaned down to peer underneath her. I looked away to give her some privacy. As if that was a thing.

"Mm-hm."

I remembered him saying he'd dated the same man on and off for years, but he didn't tell me his name. And the interviewer in me didn't want to learn the man's name and then struggle with whether or not to use it. I'd rather just not know. Which meant changing the subject, even though I was already jealous of the no-name long-term ex-boyfriend.

It would be hilarious if it wasn't my typical MO. Get crush on guy, discover he's hung up on someone he grew up with, get ditched faster than you can say "childhood sweetheart." If anything had taught me serious relationships weren't for me, it was getting ditched time and time again for the better man. But I didn't need or expect a relationship with Christian Lasley anyway. I was way out of his league. I'd be perfectly content with a little flirting and possibly a one-night stand. If there was anyone worth blurring the journalistic integrity lines for, it was Christian Lasley.

"So... I guess it's just the two of us around here tonight? Or... or are you going to leave me in the big house all by my lonesome while you sleep with the stock like a real man?" I asked.

He came out from under the horse with a knowing grin. "Might you have a preference?"

Heat pooled in my gut. I watched his hands wander over the mare and imagined them doing the same to me. "I surely do. You're looking awfully cowboy right now, Coach Lasley."

"And that does something for you, Mr. Buchanan?"

"Indeed. Your broken-in cowboy boots, the way those jeans are appreciating your assets, a barn full of fresh hay..." I blew out a breath and whistled low in my throat. "Why, I don't even need to leave the building to throw you down somewhere soft and beg you to show me how good you are with your hands."

He was so good-looking when he laughed. Relaxed, happy, confident. As powerful and intimidating as he'd always been on the field and on the sidelines, in person he was completely present and genuine. Approachable even. Now that I'd gotten past the early awkward period of being starstruck, I could see the regular guy behind the legend. No wonder his fellow players and coaches adored him and trusted him so much.

I'd known him ten seconds, and I already did too.

Christian made his way out of the stall and closed the door behind us, giving Dottie one last stroke before placing his hand on the small of my back and urging me back toward the big barn door.

"I'm going to go out on a limb and say it wouldn't be very hospitable of me to leave you in the big house all alone. What if you needed something and I wasn't there to provide it?"

"Mm. So true. Sometimes I get needy at night in a strange place."

After I walked through the open door, Christian turned and whistled. The brown and white husky left the two bigger white dogs and came running up. After giving her a scratch on the head, he closed the barn door and secured the latch behind us. When he turned back to me, his hand found mine as if it was the most natural thing in the world. We walked back side by side through the snowfall. It was coming down faster now. Our original footprints were long gone, and the edges of the walkway were almost impossible to make out. If it hadn't been for Christian, I would have probably been walking all over his lawn without realizing it.

The warm light from the house reminded me of how comfortable it had been sitting with him in the cozy den. I wanted to get back there in front of the fire and learn more about him. Flirt more with him. See that sexy-as-fuck smile light up his face when he teased me.

"You ready to finish the interview?" he asked as he opened the front door for me.

Oh, right. The interview.

I was there to work.

And I was fucking up my big break like a starstruck horndog.

"Absolutely," I said, swallowing a sigh of resignation. "Let's do it."

# 6

## CHRISTIAN

I WANTED nothing more than to seduce Hayworth into my bed and keep him there until we both suffered mild dehydration from loss of body fluids. But I owed the man the interview he'd come there to get, and I sure as hell didn't plan on letting my inappropriate attraction to him fuck up his big chance at knocking this interview out of the park. I needed to control my attraction to him—at least until after the interview was complete.

Detouring through the kitchen to start warming some soup and bread for a light dinner, I grabbed a couple of bottles of water and brought them into the den.

Hayworth sat and fiddled with his laptop while I put the mic back on before sitting back and crossing my legs to wait for the questioning to continue. Once we were underway again, the questions went much more smoothly. Hay asked the expected questions about our current season as well as more general ones like what some of my favorite memorable moments were from both playing and coaching. That portion of the interview was so easy between the two of us, it turned into a conversation in which we were trading football stories, laughing, one-upping each other with tales of crazy plays, and trying to determine which one of us had experienced the worst embarrassing moment on the field.

Finally, Hayworth glanced at his monitor and shot me wide eyes. "Well, Coach. It looks like we've far exceeded our time. Thank you so much for having me and agreeing to sit down for this fascinating and important interview. You've been a role model for many and an inspiration for me personally. Whether you were a Jackson High Bronc, a Nebraska Husker, an LA Ram, or a Denver Bronco, or a Jackson Jackal, on and off the field you've always embodied the importance of working hard, doing your best, always improving, and maintaining professionalism and sportsmanship at every challenge. Good luck against Oakland next weekend, and thank you again for your time during this busy season."

I stared at him, stunned by his kind words. "You're welcome. Thank you."

My voice sounded weird in my ears. I hoped it didn't come out as some embarrassing croak on the podcast.

Hayworth clicked a few keys before pulling out the cords and closing his laptop before setting it on the table between us. He began wrapping up the microphone cords with a huge smile on his face. "I seriously can't thank you enough. That was the interview of my dreams. Not just because of who you are, but how easy our conversation was. I think it's every journalist's goal to have an interview turn into such an easy conversation. Much more fun to listen to that kind of interplay than—"

I couldn't wait any longer. I lurched forward from my chair and grabbed his cheeks, crashing my mouth into his. He sucked in a breath of surprise, but then he was kissing me with just as much heat. His hands clutched my arms until I ran out of air and had to pull back.

"I'm sorry," I gasped. "I didn't mean to attack your face."

"Fuck. Attack my face. Please attack my face." Hayworth panted between words.

I grinned. "You're just so damned sincere and kind and... sweet.

And beautiful. I... god, Hayworth. I really want to keep touching you. I can't stop thinking about touching you."

"Yeah. Again. Do it. No complaining here. See this face?" He gestured to his face. "This is my not-complaining face."

I leaned in and dropped soft kisses along his cheek to his neck. "God, you taste amazing. But you must be starving. First I feed you. Then I feed *on* you." Hay shuddered deliciously which served to perk my dick up even more if that was possible.

I stood up and reached for his hand. "Leave all this here. I have soup on the stove and a salad in the fridge."

Hayworth followed me into the kitchen, finding Brownie right away and baby-talking her. I made my way to the stove and stirred the soup. "Do you have a dog?" I asked him.

"No. My mom had hoity-toity cats when I was growing up. I accidentally let a stray knock one of them up one time, and I wound up taking one of the kittens. So now I have Chip. But I've always been more of a dog person. Unfortunately, Chip knows it. I take it this one is yours? The ones who didn't come back with us just stay in the barn with the horses?"

"This is Brown Dog. She's been with me four years now. The Great Pyrenees work the ranch and keep an eye on the stock."

We took our dinner to the large kitchen table and sat across from each other to eat. I asked him more about growing up in Charleston, and he told me about the wealthy, country club world he'd been raised in.

"Yeah, my parents were relieved when I moved out west, and honestly, it was a relief for me too. But then I felt this weird kind of desperation to do all the gay things at once," he said with a chuckle. "I went to clubs, danced my ass off. Slept around, brunched with friends. It was amazing. But it was also overwhelming and so different from the life I'd had before. I almost think it was like having a midlife crisis at thirty instead of fifty."

Hearing him describe dancing and fucking other men made my shoulders tight for some reason. I didn't like thinking of him sleeping around with anyone and everyone. He deserved one person to take care of him, adore him. Hell, spoil him rotten. After having a shitty, unsupportive family, he deserved to have someone completely dedicated to him for once. Someone steadfast and loyal.

Someone like me.

I thought back to what I'd told Hayworth about wanting a life. This. *This* was what I'd envisioned. Meeting an interesting man and making a special connection. Sitting across from him in front of a fire on a snowy night and talking effortlessly into the night without worrying about who might find out.

There were years when I'd wanted nothing more than a hot body and a quick fuck. Just enough to slake my lust in the heat of the moment. But one evening in Hayworth's company and I wanted so much more.

"Why are you looking at me like that?" he asked with a knowing grin.

"I'm picturing you naked," I lied with a wink.

His grin widened. So sexy.

"And what do I look like?"

I stood and pulled his chair back before reaching out my hand for him to take.

"Perfection."

But in my head, I was screaming, *Mine*.

# 7

HAYWORTH

I was proud of myself for acting normal. There was an entire varsity cheer squad in my head thanking Jesus and the holy smokes for leading me to this moment in my life. As I watched Christian walk up the stairs, I realized he must still keep up with a vigorous squats routine in private. He had the exact same tight, muscular ass he'd had as a player years before.

I reached out and pinched it. "God this is glorious."

He swatted my hand away. "If you start that stuff on the stairs, we'll never make it to the bedroom."

"Who says stairs can't be fun?"

"Me. I'm too old for that shit."

He reached the top and held out his hand for mine again, bringing it to his mouth and pressing a kiss to the back of it. "Plus," he said, "you deserve better than that. I want to savor you. That can't happen if we're at the emergency vet."

I snorted. "Vet?"

"Mm-hm. It's closer than the hospital. And cheaper too."

He led me into a bedroom that was clearly kept away from public view. This was where all the good stuff was. There were trophies and jerseys, framed photos of him with all kinds of celebrities, and a giant-screen TV mounted on one wall. And, unsurprisingly, a giant-sized bed.

"That's an awfully big bed. How tall are you?" I asked out of curiosity. I was six feet and he still seemed to soar above me.

"Six four and a half. But I'm making a note of the fact you didn't have that stat memorized. You just lost some fanboy points."

Christian's fake pout was adorable, and I couldn't wait any longer to touch him everywhere. I tackled him onto the bed and kissed his fucking brains out.

"Here's your fanboy," I murmured between kisses. "Gonna fan the fuck out of you."

His laughter rumbled deeply between us. His hands were everywhere on my back, my ass, my upper thighs. He finally snuck them up under my new Nebraska sweatshirt and yanked my shirt out of my pants. Finally, finally his big warm hands were on the bare skin of my back.

"Mm-hm," I encouraged. "More of that. Hands."

"Take all this shit off."

I sat up and yanked off the sweatshirt before tackling the buttons of my shirt. Christian started at the bottom while I did the ones at the top. He kept meeting my eyes with intensity. Every look was like a promise of something hot and full of orgasms.

And I wanted whatever it was he was offering.

When my shirt was finally undone enough to shed, I yanked off the undershirt as well and reached for his own shirt. We did the same teamwork thing with his buttons until both of us were bare from the waist up and scrambling at each other's belts.

While I worked his buckle, my lips found his skin. His shoulder, his collarbone. I licked and sipped across all that honeyed expanse to the hairy chest below. Once I took a nipple into my mouth, it was over. I couldn't concentrate on the belt thing anymore. I humped his leg while pulling at his nipple with my mouth, licking and sucking more with each groan out of his throat.

Suddenly, Christian's hands were in my hair. "Come up here, beautiful," he murmured.

I moved back up, expecting to kiss him on his lips some more. Instead, the look on his face stopped me in my tracks.

"I need you to know..." he began.

Oh, shit. Was he going to tell me something personal? Was he HIV positive?

"It's okay. I'm on PrEP and we can use condoms," I said, trying to reassure him before he had to say the words.

His face softened. "No, baby. I'm negative. But—"

My brain was spinning, and I was terrified he was going to say something that would bring this whole dream to an end. Was he worried I'd run and tell everyone I'd slept with the great Christian Lasley?

"I won't tell anyone," I blurted, interrupting him. "I... I wouldn't do that to you. I'd never—"

He put a finger on my lips. "Shh. Be still for a minute and let me get this out. I don't need you to keep any secrets for me, but thank you for saying that."

I nodded, enjoying the feel of his finger on my lip.

"Hayworth, I like this. You, I mean. I like the connection we're making. I don't want you to think I just want a quick fuck. I'd like more than just tonight. And, ah, I thought you should know that."

*Well, melt my heart and pour it into a Christian Lasley–shaped mold.*

"Same," I mumbled against his finger before kissing it. "So much same."

I tried not to listen to the little voice in my head reminding me all guys say that. I was always their favorite when I was naked in their bed.

His face morphed into a sweet smile. "Really? You feel this too?"

I nodded and pulled his hand away, holding it against my chest instead. Just because I knew being with Christian would never turn into something more than casual, didn't mean I couldn't wish otherwise. So, I was honest with him. "I like you so much. The real you. The one I'm getting to know today. I promise I'm not *only* having starstruck feelings for you."

He laughed and reached for me with his free hand, pulling my face back down to his for a kiss.

"I'll take you any way I can get you," he teased. "And I'm not opposed to a little celebrity worship if it gets your pants off."

If the man wanted my pants off, my pants were coming off.

I shimmied out of those fuckers like they were on fire.

# 8

## CHRISTIAN

He was even hotter naked.

Hayworth stood and stripped the rest of the way down until he was completely on display for me in my teenage bedroom like something I'd conjured during a particularly hot jack-off session.

"Come here."

He frowned. "You seem to still have your own pants on, Coach."

Oh, right. I stripped and held both arms out to him after chucking the pants and boxer briefs across the room. "Now."

Hay came right back into my arms like he'd been made to be there. As our naked bodies slid together, both of us let out groans of pleasure. He felt so good against me. His body warmth, the friction of hair, the curves of muscle, and the scent of faded aftershave mixed with faint traces of sweat.

Hayworth Buchanan was delicious.

I flipped him onto his back and took over, mapping his body with my mouth and hands until he was writhing and begging, his legs tangled around the back of mine. After making my way lower and lower, I finally took his cock into my hand and began lapping at it to wet it fully before taking it all the way into my mouth.

"Fuck, ah! Oh, god, Chris. *Fuck*." His voice sounded breathy and out of control. I glanced up to see his head thrown back and his neck exposed. His hands grabbed at the sheets while his legs came around me again and rested on my back.

I pulled back enough to toy with just the head. When he finally looked down at me, I saw his flushed face and bright eyes.

"*Chris.*"

I loved the sound of my name on his tongue. "What do you want? How do you want to come, Hayworth? Tell me. Anything you want, just tell me."

"Face-to-face. Frot, fuck, I don't care. Just want to see you, kiss you."

I took him down my throat as deeply as I could one more time before lurching up to kiss him again. My dick slid across his saliva-slick one, answering the question of what to do. I was way too close already to even consider prep for either one of us. Instead, I reached over to my side table and fumbled open the drawer before pulling out the lube and pumping some into my hand.

Hay got his hands on my ass, pulling my cheeks apart and teasing the crease with a long finger.

"Stop," I groaned. "Can't think."

"Don't think. Feel. Feel my finger where I'm going to fuck you someday." Hayworth's finger brushed over my hole.

"*Ngh!*"

I brought the lube to our cocks with a shaking hand and slathered them up before grasping both shafts together in one hand. With the other, I continued to hold some of my weight off him so I wouldn't crush him. Hay began thrusting up into my grip, causing our dicks to push slickly against each other. It wasn't going to take long at this rate.

We basically wet-humped each other, groaning and gasping between sloppy kisses until I could barely breathe. My balls tightened a second before I felt Hay's release hit my hand.

"Oh fuck, *Hay.*" My own orgasm overtook me just as Hayworth brought his strong hand over mine and kept stroking us. I shot across his belly and chest, adding to the hot fluid that was already there.

Seeing our combined releases on him made another ripple of electricity slam through me. Our labored breathing was the only sound in the silence

I kissed him softly before moving down to kiss under his chin, nuzzling into the damp warmth there and enjoying the scents of our bodies and sex surrounding us. Hayworth's fingers sifted idly through my hair, and his legs tightened around the back of mine again.

After a minute of soft kisses and touches, Hayworth lifted my chin up with a finger and thumb until our eyes met.

"I'm not leaving your bed tonight."

My chest squeezed. *Or any night soon*, I thought stupidly. "Damned straight," I answered in a gruff voice. "I have more plans for you."

His gorgeous grin reappeared, brightening the entire room and making me feel goofy inside. "But first, I need a hose down. So maybe I spoke too soon."

After we took turns in the bathroom, we slid under the covers in my bed and found our way back into each other's arms, lying side by side so we could see each other. Once again, he pretzeled his legs with mine and then began to run his fingers through the hair on my chest. His eyes followed his fingers before looking up at me quickly and away again.

"Ask your question," I said softly. I could tell something was bothering him, but he was trying not to ask.

"The guy you dated..."

"Lane."

"Agh!" he snapped, slapping his palms over his ears. "No names!"

I reached out to pull his hands down. "You're not interviewing me right now. What about him?"

"Was he your high school sweetheart?" Hayworth looked poised to take one on the chin, like he was suddenly expecting me to admit to having a spouse and five kids.

"Does it matter?"

"I don't know. No. Of course not. Don't be silly. I mean, why would it? Heh." He sucked in a breath and blurted, "I'm sorry. Ignore me..." He moved to sit on the edge of the bed, facing away from me.

I crawled across the mattress and put my arms around him from behind, resting my chin on his shoulder. "What's happening?"

"Are you together now? I mean 'off' but you might soon be 'on' again?"

"Me and Lane?"

"Fuck. Never mind. You're right, it doesn't matter. I'm here to do an interview. This is stupid, and I'm a fucking idiot," he snapped, rolling his shoulder to shake out of my hold. "I'm going to find somewhere else to sleep."

I scrambled off the bed and came around to stand in front of him, holding on to his shoulders and stooping a little to meet his eyes.

"No, you're not. You're going to sit back down and tell me what in the world is happening in your brain. Then, if you want to sleep in the guest room, I'll show you where it is."

His jaw was set in defiance, but I could still feel the slight tremble in his body. "I'm sorry," he said gruffly. "I'm acting unprofessionally."

I looked down at our naked bodies and back up at him. "We just fucked. Unless there's cash on the nightstand I'm unaware of, professionalism doesn't enter into this."

He deflated a little. "I'm just so embarrassed. It's just one night. I should have never—"

I took him in my arms again. "Hay, relax. I am completely single. I dated Lane Young on and off for years because he was a safe, secret option. In between more exciting relationships for him, he came running back to me rather than choosing to be alone. And I took the scraps he was willing to offer."

"I'm sorry," he said. "That sounds shitty."

"Sometimes shitty scraps are better than nothing."

Hay frowned. "I don't want you to have either."

My entire chest felt warm and full. "Then stay in my bed tonight, Hayworth."

**9**

---

## HAYWORTH

MY INSECURITY HAD REVEALED itself like one of those cheesy scenes out of a horror movie where the villain rips off his fake face to show the ugliness below. *Oh, you think this is Sweet Hayworth? Surprise, it's really Kathy Bates in that movie about the guy with the feet.*

"You should seriously drop-kick me into the nearest snowy field and leave me to get eaten by horses," I muttered, settling back into Christian's bed next to him.

Chris rubbed both hands over his face. "First of all, no offense, but the horses wouldn't eat you."

"Fuck. I'm too gamey, aren't I? I need to eat more carbs."

"You're perfect—hot as fuck, actually. If I was a horse, I'd totally eat you. Which is not a sentence I ever thought I'd say. Second of all, you're allowed to be insecure when I spent twenty minutes earlier telling you about the last guy I dated like an idiot."

"I have an issue. It involves guys ditching me for their high-school true love," I admitted. "So... the thing with... Lane, well, it kinda touched a button. Sorry. It's really none of my business."

"Hay. You are naked in my bed. Tell me how my relationship status is none of your business. And what was that bullshit about it only being one night when we just had the conversation about it being more than just one night? Did you change your mind? If so, please tell me now."

"No. No, I didn't. I had a situation in which there was temporary insanity brought on by ugly insecurity, and I would appreciate it very much if we could pretend it never happened."

Christian's face softened into an understanding smile, and he reached his hand out to cup my cheek. "For the record, you have nothing to be insecure about. You are gorgeous, funny, smart, good at your job, and have a massive dick."

"You really think I'm good at my job? That wasn't just something you were saying, earlier?"

He laughed. "That's the part you want confirmation on?"

I debated whether or not to admit to something that had been bothering me. "Well, I got a callback for a job at ESPN last week, but I don't know if I should do it. I feel like I'm too inexperienced. And I'm not sure it's really what I want. But shouldn't I want it?"

Chris sat up and stared at me in surprise. "Hayworth, that's incredible. You should at least go hear what they have to say. You're really good at what you do. And you're not inexperienced, dammit. You have a journalism degree and have been running your own sports commentary programs for years. I think if you listen to what they have to say, you'll get a gut feeling for whether or not it's right. But regardless of what you decide, the content you produce is valuable. I'd think any of those sports networks would be thrilled to have you."

My eyes must have been bugging out of my head because he took one look at me and laughed.

"Babe, are you seriously still surprised that I like you and think you're pretty amazing?"

I nodded. "Uh-huh."

"C'mere." He reached out and pulled me up, encouraging me to straddle his lap so he could hug me. Considering we were both so tall, it felt a bit like two giraffes trying to figure out how to fit in an economy plane seat. There were too many arms and legs and not enough places to put them. We gave up and tumbled back down to lie side by side.

Christian's hand caressed my cheek. "I'd love to see you behind the desk at ESPN. That way I could ogle you whenever I wanted."

"You can do that anyway," I teased. I studied him, taking in the ripped abs, the messy hair, the five-o'clock shadow on his cheeks. I reached out to feel his whiskers with the tip of my finger. "Can we stop talking about work?" I asked softly. "I can't concentrate when you're lying here being so fucking hot."

Chris turned his face to kiss the tip of my finger. "Can you stay longer than one night?"

My throat thickened, but I reminded myself this wasn't the beginning of a love story. It was a casual hookup, even if he didn't realize it yet. I simply wasn't the guy you picked for the long haul. And that was okay. "Nah," I muttered. "I'll have to get home and edit the show before flying out to Minneapolis to cover a collegiate tennis thing."

"I can't argue with that... Okay, well then can we at least make some plans, because not knowing when we're going to see each other next doesn't feel great to me right now."

I frowned at him, trying to decide how much he meant what he was saying. "Yeah. Um, okay. I'd... that would be good. I'd like that."

Christian's face seemed to relax, and he leaned in to kiss me again. This time his lips moved more slowly, and he took his time teasing my mouth with his own before moving his mouth along my cheek to my ear in little nibbles.

"Sunday night. Will you come see me?" he whispered.

"Hmm? What?"

I arched up into his body until his question sank in, and I almost head-butted him when I realized what he was saying.

"You're playing Oakland!"

He lay back laughing at me. "Yes, Sunday at one. Would it freak you out if I invited you to come? I can get you a ticket or press pass if you'd rather. And you can come to my hotel room after. Think of it like doing me a favor. If I win, we can celebrate. If I lose, you can help me forget."

There wasn't a scenario on earth in which I'd turn down a chance to see him again.

"Yeah, okay. I guess so," I said with a sniff. "I mean, if it will help you. I'd be willing to do that. For *you*."

He laughed some more, trying to pull me closer, but I used the momentum to roll on top of him, quickly restraining his wrists above his head on the pillow. His laughter died down, and he gave me the intense eye contact again. I'd never felt this closely connected to someone so quickly before. Maybe it should have scared me, but it didn't.

Not at all.

# 10

## CHRISTIAN

I AWOKE in the middle of the night to hear Brownie whining at the door like she needed to go out. That was unusual for her, but I wasn't willing to take the chance since she could have an upset stomach or something. After carefully extracting myself from Hayworth's warm body, I placed a light kiss on his head and climbed out of bed to put some clothes on.

He shifted in the bedding and mumbled something into the pillow.

"Shh, go back to sleep," I whispered. "Just taking Brownie out really quick."

After throwing back on my jeans and grabbing a fleece pullover and fresh pair of thick socks from my dresser, I made my way downstairs to where my coat and boots were.

"You owe me one," I grumbled at my still-whining dog. "If you're just asking to go out because you hear something fun out there, you're in trouble."

As soon as I opened the front door, she bolted toward the barn. I followed her as quickly as I could without breaking my neck and pulled open the barn door. The two Great Pyrenees were pacing in front of Dottie's stall, and I could hear the sounds of a horse in distress. The horses in the other stalls were nervously shifting around more than usual for the middle of the night, most likely keyed in to the sounds and smells of a horse in labor.

Since she'd showed signs of waxing the night before, I wasn't too surprised to discover her preparing to foal, but I still cursed Murphy's Law for her deciding to do this while all the hands were gone. Perry was going to have a field day when he found out I was on my own for her delivery.

When I got to the stall, I saw she was pacing and agitated in a normal way. Nothing looked concerning other than the fact she was definitely in the first stage of labor.

It had been too long since I'd been present for a foaling for me to handle this on my own. I needed another set of hands and someone else around in case shit went wrong. As much as I hated to disturb poor Hayworth from his warm sleep, I was going to have to wake him up and drag him out here.

I gave Dottie a thorough check before turning around and making my way back to the house. Once back in the bedroom, I leaned in and kissed Hay's cheek with my freezing lips.

He sucked in a breath. "Jesus fuck. What did you eat? Ice burgers?"

"Winter air in Wyoming," I said. "Get up, buttercup. We have a foal to deliver."

"Huh?" He turned and squinted at me in the dim light coming from the hallway. He looked so sleepy and cute, I wanted nothing more than to slide back in the warm bed next to him.

"Dottie's in labor. It's time to grab the go bag and get to the hospital."

"Wha?"

Confused Hay was even cuter than sleepy Hay.

"That was a joke, but I need your help in the barn. I at least need a second pair of hands in case something goes wrong. And you're the only other man around here tonight besides me. The hands are gone for the night. We thought they'd be back before she delivered, but it looks like the joke's on us."

"You want me to deliver a pony?"

I brushed the hair off his forehead. "A *foal*. A pony is... you know what? Never mind. Yes, baby. I need your help delivering a pony."

He smiled at my endearment and reached for my hand before pulling it to his chest and snuggling back down under the covers like he was going back to sleep. God, he was so damned tempting.

I leaned toward his ear and took the lobe into my mouth, speaking around it. "If her labor takes a long time, I can make hay in the hay with Hay."

"Har har. Don't quit your day job," he mumbled.

"I'll say it another way. If you come to the barn and help me, I'll suck that thick cock of yours with my hot, wet mouth until your balls explode and coat my throat in your spunk."

He was whimpering before I even finished the sentence. The sound was enough to get my own dick interested, but we didn't have time right now.

"Prepayments only," he pleaded.

"No can do. The clock is ticking out in the barn. Tell you what, if you promise not to fall back asleep, I'll leave you to take your time getting dressed. I'm going to lay out a set of long underwear and warm coveralls for you. It's cold as fuck out there, so bundle up. Join me in the barn when you're dressed. We've got a coffee maker out there if you need it."

"*Grnf.*"

I leaned in for a final kiss, deepening it enough to wake him thoroughly before standing back up.

I laid out the clothes and then raced back down the stairs to return to the barn. Dottie was doing fine, so I went ahead and put coffee on. A few minutes later, a super-bulky version of Hayworth arrived, outfitted exactly how I'd told him. A few stray pieces of hair shot out from the edges of the beanie, and his eyes were still a bit squinty.

"Hey, sleepyhead. Thanks for coming. I'm sorry to make you get up."

He walked right up and leaned his head on my chest, grumbling under his breath about his balls shrinking in the early-morning cold. I kissed his head and promised to help him find them later.

"If I have to stick an arm up a horse butt, I'm out," he assured me. "You're cute, but not that cute."

"I beg your pardon. I'm irresistible."

"Meh."

He snuggled closer, and I could smell the familiar scent of my bedsheets on him.

"You know it doesn't come out of her butt, right?" I teased.

He groaned. "Can't I be the one holding her paw, or whatever, at the front and cheering her on? I can yell *push* with the best of them."

"Sure, babe. I'll let you hold her paw. Why don't you head on in there and wipe her brow too, while you're at it? I'm sure she'd love that."

He peeked into the stall and witnessed Dottie rolling around on her back in the hay, thrashing her legs in the air and grunting.

"Ahhh, on second thought... you said something about coffee? And where can I find the vagina gloves? I need size long please."

I barked out a laugh. "No vagina for you. Dick only. C'mon. Let's get you some caffeine. If this is you without caffeine, we're going to have fun once you get juiced up."

We got coffee and chatted while sitting on a deep bench built into the wall next to the stall door. Every few minutes, I'd peek in on Dottie to make sure she wasn't showing signs of unusual distress. She seemed to be progressing normally and only needed my help keeping the stall clean and dry.

I asked Hayworth a ton of questions about his podcast and blog. He told me how it had started off as a radio show in college.

"Yeah, one of my professors announced the college radio station was looking for some people do to talk shows. They had plenty of students interested in being a DJ, but not enough doing other things like news, human-interest stories, stuff like that. So I figured what the hell? It was worth extra credit in that professor's class, and by then football season was over. Man, I loved it. All I did was riff on whatever games had been played that week. I reported scores, interesting plays, little fun facts about the players and coaches."

"Is that what you'd set out to do? Did you know you wanted to go into media?"

"Hell no. I went to school for sports management. But once I got into the radio show, I switched to journalism. It made my dad crazy. He'd already mentally cast me in the movie Jerry Maguire and imagined I'd be taking him along to all the big games and introducing him to all the celebrities."

"Didn't he realize you could do the same thing as a high-level journalist in the sport?"

Hay rolled his eyes. "I mean, sure. But what were the chances of me getting high level in either career?"

I blinked at him and then gestured to myself. "You got a callback with ESPN. Hell, you scored an exclusive interview with the uber-handsome Christian Lasley of the Jackson Jackals."

"You don't count. Admit it. You only picked me for my big dick."

"Yes, because I have X-ray vision. Through a podcast. Although... it *is* a big dick. Show it to me again so I can make sure I'm remembering correctly."

Hayworth stood up with a cheeky grin and started unzipping his coveralls in front of my face. Instead of stopping him, I helped. Once his coveralls were open, I reached in and fished out his cock from inside the soft long-underwear, noting how warm he was and how deliciously musky he smelled.

I pulled him closer and took his cock into my mouth, looking up at his face and meeting his eyes while I began sucking it. There was so much affection in his face, I felt it in my chest. I ran a free hand up the outside of his thick coveralls and left it on his chest. He covered it with his own and used the other to cup the back of my head gently as I worked over his cock. His expression quickly turned from tender to tense as his orgasm built until he was grunting out a warning. I reached both hands around to clutch his ass and keep him from pulling out.

He shot long and hot in my throat, crying out my name and grabbing my hair. Seeing him come apart like that, in the barn that was usually full of gruff cow hands and ranch work made it seem almost otherworldly. Like we were in our own little bubble, which in a way I guessed we were.

"Damn, cowboy," he said when he caught his breath. "You do mighty fine with that mouth of yours."

After tucking him back in his clothes and fastening everything for him, I stood up and kissed him. His arms came around me and tried pulling me close, but the combination of both our winter gear made it next to impossible.

Hayworth pulled away laughing. "You're being cockblocked by your damned coat. Serves you right for not living someplace warmer."

I tried adjusting my still-stiff cock in a way Hay couldn't see. Not only did I need to check on the mare, but I also didn't want Hayworth to think he owed me anything.

Dottie was in the second stage of labor, so I forced myself to focus on her instead of Hayworth. When I could see the foal's hoof sticking out through the amnion, I yanked him closer to look. "That's a hoof. It's coming."

"Holy cow! This is incredible."

Hay stood at my shoulder and watched as Dottie rolled around grunting periodically. It was a messy process, but eventually, the baby was out and Dottie was sniffing and nosing it.

"Oh my god, Christian. That's a brand-new horse. That giant thing came out of poor Dottie."

Our hands were clasped tightly together without me realizing it. "It sure did. Looks like a colt, but I'm not completely sure. We'll know better in a few hours. Meanwhile we'll let Dottie clean him up and keep an eye on them."

Hayworth watched, mesmerized, as Dottie continued her attentions on the new baby. After a while, Dottie stood up and shook herself off. I took the opportunity to clean out as much of the mess as I could and replace it with dry bedding, asking Hay for help keeping Dottie's attention away from me. We made another pot of coffee and sat back down on the bench to keep an eye on the pair a little longer.

Conversation between the two of us came easy. We talked about anything and everything—football, travel, growing up, relationships, ranching, college, the fact all our friends seemed to be settling down. With Hayworth, time seemed to speed up, and before we knew it, several more hours had passed.

"You getting hungry?" I asked. It was probably past sunrise.

"Yeah, you?"

I nodded. It was the first time things had felt a little awkward between us. Suddenly, I remembered sunrise brought with it a new day.

The day Hayworth was scheduled to fly away from me. He'd only been there less than a day, and I already knew I wanted more of him.

Way more.

# 11

## HAYWORTH

Leaving the warmth of Christian's arms in the cold of Wyoming and returning to my little apartment in the city was pitiful. It seemed even dinkier and lonelier than before. Which was saying a lot. But the one thing that made it easier to say goodbye to Christian had been knowing I'd see him in Oakland the following weekend. In the meantime, I vowed to work hard in order to help the time pass.

The next day, in my best effort to ignore the lovesick pang in my gut, I threw myself into editing the interview. There were hours of conversation recorded, so it wasn't easy to pare it down to a smaller selection. Of course, hearing Christian's voice in my headset made my chest tight and my dick hard, so it was a bit like trying to work all day while simultaneously doing your best not to masturbate at your desk.

I wasn't entirely successful.

After several hours, I couldn't keep from texting him. We'd talked on the phone the night before when I'd gotten home, but we'd eventually had to hang up so he could get some sleep for his big work-week ahead.

Listening to your voice is making this editing job a total bitch.

CHRISTIAN

At least you get to hear mine. I don't even
have that. BTW Dottie's baby is definitely a
colt. We named him Buchanan. The hands
are calling him Buck.

No way! OMG, can I tell people you were so
impressed by my sexual abilities, you named
a stallion after me?

CHRISTIAN

Sure, just show them the pic of your 'stallion'
when you do.

A picture of the tiny, leggy colt came through. He stood
awkwardly like he didn't know what to do with so many limbs. The
little guy was precious, but strong and virile yet, he was not.

I laughed out loud.

Way to make a guy feel powerful. But that's
still a fine-looking foal.

CHRISTIAN

You should see him with milk on his face.
Cutest fucking thing.

You made your point. I'm a child. I get it.

CHRISTIAN

Nah, if you were a child, that would make me
a super-perv.

Busy day for you today?

CHRISTIAN

Yeah, meetings and practice.

The conversation felt flirty but also domestic. I loved picturing
him at work, smiling down at his phone between meetings with the
team. It almost felt like we were dating. But the idea of dating him
was ridiculous, and I had to remind myself that one of the reasons
he'd finally come out was to be able to live as a gay man. For many

guys, that included playing the field. And why shouldn't he? He was gorgeous and fit, successful and fairly famous. I could just imagine the fun he could get up to now that he didn't have to worry about someone finding out.

I'd gone through a similar phase once I'd moved to California, and I'd loved the hell out of it. Why wouldn't he deserve the same kind of fun? I could hardly blame him for not wanting to jump right out of his relationship with Lane into another one with someone else. But was I willing to see him again, knowing it wasn't going to progress to something more serious? And what happened if someone saw me with him and thought we were an item? Would it mess up his chances to see other people?

*I should cancel.*

I'd thought about this off and on since leaving the ranch the day before, but I hadn't been able to bring myself to ask him about it. I brought up his contact info and hit Send to start a call.

"Hey, beautiful," Christian said. I closed my eyes and drank in the sound of him.

"Hey, yourself."

"I'd like to *Hay* myself," he said with a chuckle. "But you'd have to get your ass back here for that to happen."

"Um, I know you're busy, but I wanted to ask you something about this weekend."

"Whatever it is, the answer is yes."

My gut flipped upside down with nerves. "I think maybe I shouldn't come to the game?" It came out as more of a question than a statement.

Silence came from the other end, so I rushed to fill it.

"Because... well, you're... you know... *you*, and busy. It's going to be crazy, and what if someone sees us togeth—"

"Are you worried about me, baby?" he asked in a soft voice. "Because that's making me miss you even more than I already do."

The endearment made my stomach flip, but I tried not to take it as a sign of any real feelings on his part. "I just don't want to make things weird for you or put any pressure on you. I don't want the press to think just because we're together that means we're dating, you know?"

"The media's going to do what they do. I'm not going to worry about them. Hayworth, I want you there. Not a doubt in my mind. But what do you want?"

My stomach flipped at the sound of him not hesitating. "Um, same. Without a doubt, I want to be there. So... okay. If you're sure."

"I am. And have I told you yet that you are the sweetest man alive and I miss you already?"

"No," I said. "Do go on."

"You've been gone just over twenty-four hours and my dick is already sore from, ah, self-flagellation." He'd lowered his voice as if making sure no one could hear him talking dirty to me.

"Same here," I admitted. "It's bad. I might need medical attention. Or at least some salve."

"You'd better lay off a few days before I see you. I'm going to need that monster in prime fighting condition."

I rubbed said "monster" through my pants to reassure it that real, third-party human relief was less than a week away. I could make it that long. Couldn't I?

"Chris?" I asked. There must have been something funky in my voice.

"You okay?"

I nodded stupidly, as if he could see me through the phone. "Yeah. I wanted to make sure you knew that... ah..." I let the words drift off, unsure of where I'd been going with that.

"Yeah," he said softly. "Me too. I can't wait to see you."

I let out a breath. "Call me later?"

"If not sooner."

**12**

———

CHRISTIAN

I was like a silly kid with a crush. It reminded me of this one woman who used to wait outside the training facility for our punter. The woman had such a big crush on Matt, you could practically see the hearts float out of her eyes when she caught sight of him. She never approached him—simply waved and blushed, stammered a shy hello, and then left.

That was how I felt about Hayworth Buchanan after only one night with the man. It was ridiculous. Every time I saw his name come up on my text app or caller ID, I felt my heart race and my face heat.

While we were getting ready for the game on Sunday, Hayworth texted to let me know he'd picked up his ticket and press pass with no problems. After the text, he added an emoji of a smiley face blowing a kiss.

Just knowing he was in the same stadium as I was made me happy.

I typed back a response, asking him if they'd given him the Jackals hoodie to wear too. Grinning like a fool, I added the little fox emoji I always used to represent a jackal.

"Why you making love to that phone?"

I looked up at KJ Toole, who, despite being one of the toughest defensive backs in the league, had a notorious mischievous streak. "No reason," I said, knowing full well the grin was still there and I was most likely blushing.

He turned back to a cluster of his teammates finishing getting their gear together. "Coach got a fish on the hook," he called out with a big grin. A group of whoops and whistles rang out, accompanied by laughter and lewd comments.

"It a guppy or a hammerhead, Coach?" one of my linemen asked. "Maybe a spearfish, if you know what I mean."

"I think you mean swordfish," someone corrected with a laugh.

More whoops. I heard someone mumble something about a "rainbow fish" under their breath, but I chose to ignore it. For the most part the team had been surprisingly respectful and supportive since I'd come out a few weeks earlier.

"More like a gorgeous blue whale," I said with a grin. "Now, mind your business and let's get to work. There's a field full of Raiders waiting to get their asses handed to them. Tell you what, you bring home the win and I might introduce you to him after the game. How's that?"

The confirmation of me having someone special made the volume in the crowded room grow to a crescendo before the players finally changed their chanting and teasing to the game ahead before filing out of the locker room and into the tunnel.

The game was ugly, but we finally got our act together late in the second half and secured the win with some stellar stamina by our defense. Once we were back in the locker room, I praised the defensive line for staying strong all the way to the whistle.

"Now we gonna get to meet your man, Coach?" someone asked.

"He's not my man, Deke. At least not yet."

Deke shot me a wink. "Aww, we'll help you close the deal. Get him in here."

I noticed a few of the journalists doing locker room interviews turn their heads at the banter. The last thing I wanted was to put Hayworth in the media spotlight too soon, so I texted him to ask him to wear his press badge when he came in. Maybe if the other reporters saw him in a press badge, they'd just assume he was another journalist rather than my... whatever he was.

When he finally found his way to where we were, I wanted nothing more than to gather him up in a giant hug and hold him tight. But I was leery of scaring him off with too much too soon.

"Hay," I said, probably grinning from ear to ear. "You made it."

He looked nervous but smiley, and I was hit in the gut again by how fucking hot he was. I was surprised the room full of people hadn't dropped their jaws the minute he'd walked in.

I knew if I did anything other than shake his hand in a room so full of gossips and media, there would be photos of us embracing plastered all over the internet within second. So I reached out to shake his hand, locking eyes with him in hopes of communicating how much I'd rather the handshake be a full-body grope.

As soon as our palms touched, I grabbed tightly and held on, bringing my other hand up to encompass our grip. Our eyes met. "I'm so glad you're here," I said softly.

He blushed and looked away. "Me too. Good win out there, Coach." He pulled his hand out of my grip but stayed close. "For a minute I thought Marshawn Lynch was going to get the better of you. I should have known better."

My stomach warmed with the reminder that he spoke my language. A sexy gay man who was into me *and* understood the challenge of defending against the run? I wanted to get him back to the hotel and beg him to fuck me right this minute.

Hard.

"Yeah, well, I promised the team if they brought home the win, I'd introduce them to the famous Hayworth Buchanan from Hay Sports."

His eyes widened in surprise. "Really?"

I nodded and turned to the cluster of guys closest to where we stood. "Guys, this is the whale I told you about. Hayworth Buchanan. He did the—"

KJ cut me off, stepping forward to shake Hay's hand. "The interview. You're the podcaster, right?"

"That's right," Hay said. "Nice to meet you, KJ. Good job on that sack in the first quarter. I was hoping you'd do it again in the second."

KJ's grin turned to a pout. "Me too, goddammit. Ain't like I didn't try. Slippery motherfucker."

Hay barked out a laugh. "No kidding. Next time, yeah?"

KJ tilted his head and smiled. "Did Coach pay you to say that?"

Hay's eyes flicked toward me, and I wanted to grab his hand and lay claim to him in front of everyone.

"Nah, I just know what he's thinking. And obviously, he wants you to put every quarterback on the ground as often as possible."

A few more guys from the team wandered up to meet Hayworth and join in the ribbing. It seemed like the other journalists took it at face value: just another member of the press interacting with members of the team after the game.

When the rest of the media personnel left, I finally pulled Hay into the small office off the locker room and closed the door.

Then I shoved him against the door and kissed his fucking brains out.

# 13

## HAYWORTH

I couldn't think with his hot mouth on mine.

"Mrgh," I gurgled, at least wanting him to know I approved.

"I want to get you naked," he growled. "Right fucking now."

I thought of the fifty-three muscle-bound professional football players on the other side of the closed door and shoved Christian off me.

"Fuck no. No." I sucked in a breath. "No naked." I held out a hand to keep him from attacking my face again, but not because I didn't want it. Because I sure as hell did.

Christian's eyes darkened. "Yes naked."

"Not here!" I squeaked. "Not now."

His intense stare softened into a smile. "Okay, fine. Let's get back to the hotel though, because I'm not going to be able to wait much longer. I've been fantasizing about you all week."

My stomach flipped. "Same here. But you can't look at me like that when we're in front of the team. I'll have to boner-limp through the hallways."

"Boner-limp?" One side of his mouth curved up, and I wanted to lick it.

"Yeah. It happens when I look at you and then have to walk anywhere," I muttered, reaching down to adjust myself.

Chris stepped forward again and cupped my dick. I let out a moan before I could stop myself.

"It's because of this giant cock. Which I want. In my ass. Tonight."

Blood pooled south, and I realized I wasn't going to be flaccid again until the Jackal team jet returned to Wyoming air space some-time tomorrow.

"I... I..." I stammered, trying not to arch my hips toward him and failing. "O-okay. Yeah. Yes. Mm-hm. Me fuck you."

The deep rumble of his laugh washed through me, making me even harder. But it also made my knees wobble a little too.

"You're so sweet, Hayworth. I want to eat you up." His voice was like honey dripping all over my body.

"Stop," I begged. "You're killing me."

Christian leaned forward and kissed me softly just under my ear before whispering, "I am the luckiest man in the world right now. Thank you for coming to see me."

"Uh-huh."

"You ready to go to the hotel now, baby?"

"Uh-huh."

He leaned in for another kiss, this one so soft and tender, it was almost enough to make me blurt out silly words about falling and shit. But I was able to pull back and bite my tongue just in time.

After all, he hadn't even wanted the team to know we were together. Which was fair, since we weren't. Not really. He'd told me one of his goals had been to be free and open with his sexuality, so obviously if he'd thought I was someone special he wouldn't have just offered me a handshake.

Not that I minded, because I didn't.

And I was also a liar.

I blew out a breath and tried to think de-boner thoughts. All it took was imagining any one of the linemen outside the door giving me a beatdown and my dick fell right in line.

"Let's go," I said.

When we walked back out to the locker room, most of the players had already left to find the team buses. Christian gathered his personal messenger bag and led me out of the locker room with a hand on my lower back. As soon as he placed his warm hand there, I immediately regretted what I'd thought previously about him not claiming me. Maybe that had just been in front of the media.

Sure enough, when we made our way out of the stadium and headed toward the coach at the front of the line of buses, Christian reached for my hand and threaded his fingers through mine like it was the most natural thing in the world.

I marveled at how brave he was. I'd had a few years' head start in becoming more comfortable with simple PDA, but I still knew it couldn't have been easy for him in front of his team. I squeezed his hand in support, causing him to turn and wink at me.

The man hadn't gotten to where he was today by being timid or hesitant. He'd always been a badass and a go-getter. He had multiple Super Bowl rings and a Heisman trophy for god's sake.

As we entered the coach and took our seats, several players shouted out cheers or teased him.

"How come I can't bring some sugar home, Coach?" one player asked.

I buried my face in my hands.

"Because you failed to make the catch when Andy tossed you a gimme," Chris called back.

One of his receivers piped up. "I caught six passes, Coach. You gonna find me a girl to bring back?"

"Nah," Chris called back. "But I'll find you a man. How's that?"

The chorus of "*ooh*'s" and "*burn*'s" was deafening. I almost waited for a snarky comment by a gay player taking advantage of the offer. But I remembered the reality that even if there was a gay player considering it on that bus, he was not likely to choose this moment to come out in front of his team.

Still, the teasing and joking continued the entire way into the city until the buses pulled up to the St. Regis Hotel.

Christian had held my hand on his lap the entire way there, his thumb tracing the back of my hand even when he was busy chatting with his general manager across the aisle. It was something a boyfriend would do, and I allowed myself to believe, if only for the night, that's what this was.

**14**

---

CHRISTIAN

I WASN'T AS calm as I seemed. I was happy of course, but I was still nervous about how people would respond to my being so open and affectionate with another man in their presence. It wasn't like going from years of hiding my sexuality to being out in the open was any kind of cakewalk. It was nerve-racking at best, terrifying at most.

My bigger fear was for Hayworth. I knew he'd experienced the same kind of conservative upbringing I had, and we'd both understood that coming out would cost us relationships with people we thought had our backs. The two of us had spoken about it on the phone before tonight's game, what we were comfortable with and how we both wanted to be open and confident role models to others.

But it wasn't easy. Feeling Hay's hand shake a little in my own grasp made my heart hurt. While I knew he wanted to live his life openly and not be afraid to embrace his sexuality in public, I also knew it went against years of ingrained stealth and secrecy. For both of us.

I was surprised to see Steve, the GM, introduce himself to Hayworth with a genuine smile and handshake. He praised Hay on his handling of the podcast and even chatted him up about previous episodes. I could tell my boss was making an effort, and I truly appreciated it.

The drive took forever into the city, and when we finally arrived at the hotel, I was ready to be away from everyone else and alone with Hayworth. We raced through the throngs of people in the lobby and made our way up to my room.

The minute the door to the suite closed behind us, I had him pushed up against the back of the door the way I had in the locker room office.

"Oh my god, take off your clothes," I groaned before taking his mouth in mine. I'd been fantasizing about this moment all week. "Want you naked. Want you inside of me. Please, Hay."

His hands grasped the back of my head and one of his legs wrapped around the back of mine.

"Mm-hm," he agreed. "Want to suck you first."

Christ, I wasn't going to last. After the stress of the game, and the adrenaline rush of the victory, I was primed and ready to blow. I wanted him to fuck me without mercy and come deep inside of me.

Hayworth wrestled my shirt off and dropped to his knees, reaching to unbuckle my belt. As soon as my pants were open and my dick was out, he looked up at me with a cheeky grin. "Did someone do a little manscaping this week?"

"I had high hopes for some action. Last week I wasn't prepared."

I threaded my fingers through his hair and brushed my thumb across his cheek. He turned and took the digit into his mouth, sucking it down without taking his eyes off mine.

The man was so fucking hot; I wasn't sure if maybe I'd come all over his neck before he even took me in his mouth.

"Please," I breathed.

He released my thumb and teased the head of my cock with his tongue before taking it into his mouth. The wet warmth felt like heaven.

"Fuck yeah, just like that," I sighed.

Hay's hands continued shoving my pants and boxer briefs down out of the way so his hands could move up and down the expanse of my long legs while he continued to suckle my dick.

"Take your clothes off, Hay," I begged. "Want to see you."

His hands left my legs and his warm mouth left my cock. He ripped off his clothes as fast as he could before pulling me toward the bed. "Supplies?" he asked.

The sight of his naked, muscular ass was fogging my brain. "Uh-huh."

"Get them?"

"Huh?" I looked up at his face. He'd stopped next to the bed and was grinning at me.

"Condom. Lube. Grab them, babe."

"Fuck," I said, shaking my stupor off. "Bathroom."

I took a quick detour and tossed the supplies down before pushing him onto the bed and climbing on top of him. "God, Hayworth," I said, leaning in to kiss him some more. "Want you so much."

His arms and legs came around me, and we humped against each other while we kissed. He finally moved down to prep me, sucking my dick while stretching me with lubed fingers. It felt so good, but my body resisted.

"Oh fuck," I hissed. "I haven't done this for a while."

"Bottomed?"

"Anal."

He pulled away from me and moved back up until we were face-to-face. "Chris, we don't have to—"

I didn't even let him get the words out.

"Fuck me, Hay. I want it. Badly. But prep is good." I grinned. "Lots of prep. Aggressive prep."

He kissed me again through his laughter. "Got it. Fingerfuck the hell out of you but don't let you come."

I threw my head back when his fingers entered me again. "Jesus fuck! That's good. More."

He edged me with his fingers on my gland and his mouth on my cock until I was gasping and begging for him to fuck me. Watching him take pleasure in making me crazy was incredible. It was miles away from what sex had become with Lane before our last breakup. It had never been this passionate, but in the last several years, it hadn't even been very interactive. It was more about coming and less about making each other feel good. I hoped to never get that way with Hayworth for as long as I was lucky enough to be with him.

He moved up my body, kissing a trail from my dick to my chest to my collarbone. When he finally nuzzled into my neck, Hay's arms came around me and hooked under my shoulders. I wrapped my legs around him and arched into him.

"Baby," I breathed. "Want to feel you inside me. Please."

I pulled my legs back and tilted my pelvis up in invitation. He pulled back enough to hold me behind the knees and press himself against my hole, pushing in slowly and watching my face for any discomfort. He was attentive and thoughtful, which made my chest squeeze.

Hayworth's skin was honey gold with a pink flush up his chest and neck and red beard burn along one shoulder and cheek. His eyes were glassy, and his lips were wet with my kisses. I'd never seen a hotter picture and hoped I never forgot it.

As he entered me, my body squeezed him tight and his eyes fell closed for a brief moment.

"Chris," he moaned.

"C'mere," I said, reaching for his face with one hand and pulling him close for more kisses. His mouth was sweet and soft, a contradiction to the hard, athletic body above me. We kissed as he pushed deeper into me until my body held him tightly as deep as he could go. His hips pressed down on the back of my thighs, and one of his hands came around to hold the back of my head as he moaned into my mouth.

Hayworth felt amazing. He slid one arm under my waist to hold me close and curled the other under my shoulder. As he thrust into me, I felt his lower belly brushing along my sac. Everything about him turned me on until I felt like every single nerve ending was lit up and waiting to explode in fiery sparks around us.

I quickly moved to stroke myself off, feeling the wetness at my tip and sliding it around my cock to smooth the way. Before I could begin to stroke, he moved my hand away and replaced it with his own, pumping my cock in the same rhythm of his thrusts. I whimpered into his mouth and chanted *please, please*.

My heart was full of feelings for Hayworth. Affection, attraction, pride, pleasure... but most of all gratitude. I felt so fucking lucky I was there with him in that moment.

And it was with that thought and a final tight stroke of my cock that I began to come.

**15**

———

HAYWORTH

Topping Christian Lasley? Well, that was a bucket list item I hadn't known was in the realm of possibility before tonight. And feeling his body hot and naked underneath me was something I wouldn't ever forget. His reaction to my touch, his ability to make me feel special just from the look on his face... God. It was enough to make me crave more. More of him, more of this.

After I had shot long and hard deep inside him, I lay gasping and shaking, trying not to put my full weight on him.

"Holy fuck," I wheezed as I pulled out. "Jesus."

I quickly disposed of the condom and grabbed some tissues while Christian stayed happily in his postorgasmic stupor. I cleaned us both off before sliding back beside him in bed. After a minute, he turned on his side and gazed at me while I was still sucking in air.

"You're beautiful, Hayworth." He smoothed a hand over my jaw and pushed the damp hair off my skin. "So hot and sweet."

"Gnfh."

His face cracked into a big smile. "I think that's what you said when we first met."

I put my hands over my face. "So embarrassing. But you're stupidly attractive. And tall. And... football-y."

"Football-y, huh? Good to know."

His smile was affectionate and his hand continued to pet me, brushing my hair back, stroking down the side of my face and neck. It felt amazing.

"I'm fuck drunk," I confided sleepily. "Don't tell anyone."

"Come back with me to Jackson this week," he said.

It took me a minute to realize what he'd said. My eyes widened and my stupor began to clear.

"What?"

"I'll pay for your ticket. You can work from the ranch. Please?"

I could see a sliver of insecurity in his face as if afraid I wouldn't want to come. "Are you serious?"

"Of course I'm serious. I can't... when you're here and I'm there... I can't stop thinking about you. I just want to come home from work and have you there. I know that's moving fast, Hayworth. I know it. But... just... just this week would you maybe consider it?"

I thought about his Patriots game the following week and the pressure he'd be under at work. And then I thought about having the chance to help him forget about it at night. It was tempting.

But I'd landed the interview at ESPN and I was scheduled to fly out the following day. And I knew better than to make decisions based on a simple crush. A crush didn't pay the bills or grow my business. And there was a very annoying voice in the back of my head that kept reminding me a crush wasn't the same as a relationship. Part of me still fully believed he would eventually decide to go back to his long-term relationship—the man he had years of history with.

In my experience, it was what people did. And who could blame them?

"I can't."

His face fell before I could continue. "I understand."

"No," I said, pulling him close against me. "You don't. I got that interview. I'm flying out tomorrow."

Christian's face brightened. "Really? Good for you, Hay. That's fantastic."

I shrugged. "I'm trying not to get too excited about it. There's a big difference from my weekly wrap-up to a segment on ESPN."

We talked about the possibilities of working for the network and what a move to Connecticut would be like for me. As soon as I mentioned Connecticut though, I sensed a tension in Christian's body that wasn't there before.

"Would you have to move? You couldn't broadcast from California?" he asked.

"I live in a tiny studio apartment, and it's a television network, not radio."

"Yeah, but... what... what if..." He sighed. "Never mind. I'm really excited for you, Hayworth. That's an incredible opportunity."

Our conversation petered out after that, but our hands still spoke volumes to each other for long minutes after, running fingertips over warm skin and mapping each other's bodies. We eventually fell asleep wrapped around each other like tangled cords.

When an alarm went off the next morning, I opened my eyes to a slice of bright light forcing its way through a gap in the curtains.

A strong arm tightened around my chest and a hairy leg pressed between my own, nudging up underneath my balls. My stomach swooped when I remembered who was in bed with me.

Warm lips dragged along the skin on my back.

"Please," I whispered.

"Please, what? What do you want?" His voice was gruff with sleep, and just the sound of it made me hard.

I reached up to take his hand and put it on my cock. "You touching me." His fist closed around me and stroked slowly—too slowly. I arched into him. "Do you want to fuck me?"

"Hell yes, but I have to go meet the bus," he murmured into the back of my hair. "Not enough time."

I turned over and climbed on top of him. "Do you think we have time for a quick sixty-nine?"

Chris's sleepy face lit up. "Hell yeah. Get your dick up here."

I scrambled around and started licking him, tasting the hotel soap from the midnight shower we'd shared after our second round of orgasms. He smelled so damned good and felt warm and furry under my hands. His curvy leg muscles contracted as I ran a hand over them and smoothed my palm around to cup his ass cheek.

When he sucked me down, I whimpered around his cock. The warmth of his mouth and the pull of his lips were enough to make me lose focus.

Needless to say, it didn't take long for both of us to come, and by the time we stepped out of another shower, I felt awake and refreshed.

"God," I said as I finished putting on the clean outfit I'd stashed in my messenger bag. "Maybe I should cancel the interview and come to your place after all. That's a fucking great way to start the day."

He looked over at me from where he was doing up his own pants. "Oh yeah? You thinking about sending me off to work happy?"

I winked at him. "You wouldn't be the only one happy."

"Would I be putting you on the spot if I asked you to come the following week, after the Patriots game?"

I looked up from where I'd been gathering my things and stowing them back in my bag. "For real?"

"Well, like I said, I don't want you to feel any pressure. But if you arrange your flight to arrive around the same time ours does, you won't even need to rent a car."

"That's the least of my concerns. I wouldn't want to be in the way of your workweek..."

Christian came over to me and slid his arms around my waist, pulling me in for a quick kiss. "Not in the way. I have Wi-Fi at the house and you can work while I'm gone each day. If the weather's decent, I can even get you on a horse."

"Fuck, Chris. I thought you were trying to talk me into this, not out of it," I joked.

We left the hotel room and got into the elevator, teasing each other and chatting while I searched my phone for an airplane ticket to Jackson. As more people got on the elevator, I was pushed back until Chris pulled me against his chest and wrapped an arm around my front, glancing over my shoulder at the flight times.

"Pick that one," he said, pointing to one I assumed landed close to the time his did. "Then I won't have to wait at the airport for you."

"I told you I can rent a car. I don't mind."

He kissed the side of my head. "That's almost an hour in the car without your company? No, thanks."

I caught the eye of a woman next to us who smiled and winked at me. "He's a keeper," she said.

My face heated, but I nodded. "No kidding. You should see him catch a football."

Chris chuckled behind me while the woman looked back up at him, belatedly realizing he looked like a professional athlete if for nothing other than his height.

The woman's husband turned to look at who his wife was ogling when he must have recognized Chris.

"Holy crap. You're Christian Lasley." His eyes flashed to Chris's arm around my stomach and back up at his face. I squirmed to get out of Chris's hold, but he tightened his arm to keep me there.

"I am. And this is my boyfriend, Hayworth Buchanan. He's the man behind the Hay Sports podcast. If you haven't heard of it, you should look it up."

The man seemed a mixture of uncomfortable and starstruck. "Yeah, man. I've heard of it. Nice to meet you both."

The man continued to ramble on to Chris about the Raiders game, the football season in general, and the Jackals' chances at another Super Bowl run, but as the elevator descended, all I could hear was the word *boyfriend* echoing happily in my ears.

Until we exited the elevator and began making our way toward the lobby and the sound of a million cameras clicked in our ears. For a split second, I'd felt the nervous tumble in my stomach that accompanied stark fear at accidentally outing someone against their will.

But then Chris had hugged me to his side and pressed a kiss to my temple.

"Not hiding, remember?" he murmured into my skin.

I looked up and smiled. He wasn't afraid of being seen with me.

# 16

## CHRISTIAN

When we arrived at the ranch together a week later, I was happier than I'd been in a very long time. We'd squeaked out a win against the Patriots in overtime the day before, and I was finally able to put my hands on Hayworth Buchanan after a weeklong drought.

He'd rushed straight into my arms as soon as we'd spotted each other at the airport, and I'd been excited and relieved to see him claim me so publicly.

Despite lengthy bedtime video calls every night, I felt like some distance had grown between us. When we weren't together in person, I sensed Hayworth's insecurities getting the better of him. I couldn't wait to spend an entire week reassuring him of my strong feelings.

"Show me this stallion, Coach," he teased, as we parked next to the barn. "My namesake."

I was happy to see him smiling when we ducked into the barn to check on little Buck.

"Aww, look at him, Chris," Hayworth said, turning with an adorable smile on his face. "He's so fuzzy."

"This isn't the best time of year for foaling, but it is awfully cute when their coat fluffs up in the cold," I agreed. "He loves the fresh air, which is good because Dottie insists on getting her outside time."

I showed him how to give Dottie a treat and get close enough to Buck to scratch him on the head. Dottie made a sound right when Hayworth touched Buck, and I thought Hay was going to faint dead away.

"It's okay," I said, laughing. "She's just trying to get attention for another carrot. She's not upset."

"Are you going to make me learn to ride while I'm here?" he asked.

"Do you want to learn to ride?"

Hay stepped in front of me and pressed his body against my front. "There're other things around here I'd love to ride, Coach."

I heard one of the hands a few stalls down suddenly call out, "La la la. You're burning my eardrums over there. Corrupting the innocent at the very least, boss."

Hay jumped away from me in surprise, which only made me laugh harder. I called out to Jared, "Wasn't me. And if you're so innocent, how come I saw Van Ewing's pickup parked at the bunkhouse the other night?"

"Fuck," he muttered. "You weren't supposed to see that, nosy bastard. Mind yer business."

"Lay off my man, and I might cut you some slack," I said.

"He's gay?" Hayworth mouthed.

I nodded and grinned. "Very," I mouthed back.

"What does that even mean?" he asked softly.

"Let's get to the house, and I'll show you."

It wasn't until we walked out of the barn that I noticed a familiar vehicle in the drive. My stomach fell.

"Hay, I need to warn you—"

We were cut off by the front door of the house opening and Lane calling out. "There you are. Finally."

Hayworth's hand tightened instinctively in mine as he took in the sight of a stranger coming out of my house.

Lane looked Hayworth up and down before narrowing his eyes at me. "I'd ask you who this is, but I believe every news outlet in America has already shoved that photo in my face."

In the most famous photo from the hotel, I'd had my arm around Hayworth and was pressing a kiss to his temple. Hay was looking at the ground with a shy smile and pink cheeks while my eyes were alight with happiness. There was no doubt it was a photo of two people very into each other, and I'd had to force myself not to make it my phone lock screen as soon as I'd seen it.

Hayworth slowed to a stop. "Uh, maybe I should..." He turned back toward the barn as if it could offer safety from the ugly confrontation ahead. "I can just wait in the—"

"Absolutely not. Don't be ridiculous," I said before turning my glare on Lane. "What are you doing here?"

I felt Hay's hand begin to shake in my grip, so I squeezed it in reassurance and pulled him a little closer to me.

"I need to talk to you. In private."

As we got closer, I could see Lane had been crying. My heart went out to him, because I knew him well enough to know he wasn't prone to tears.

"What's wrong?"

We continued into the house, and Hay let go of my hand long enough to kick his boots off into the tray by the door. He turned to me. "I'm going to help myself to some coffee and go hang out in the den. Take your time, okay?"

I met his eyes and felt such overwhelming gratitude for his understanding. I leaned in and pressed a kiss to his cheek. He smelled good enough to eat. "Thank you."

After Hay disappeared toward the kitchen, I gestured for Lane to head in the opposite direction to the big open living room. He took a seat on the large sofa, so I sat in one of the chairs.

"Are you okay? Did something happen? Is it your parents?"

Lane shook his head, his usually well-styled hair flopping in his face. "I don't get it, Christian. We were together for years, *years*, and you never came out. And now here's this guy you've barely known at all and suddenly you're on the fucking internet with your arm around him in front of the whole world."

"I didn't come out for him, Lane. Hell, I didn't even meet him until a couple weeks later."

"I think we should try again."

I stared at him. "You're the one who broke up with me. Every single time. And never once did you even hint at wanting me to come out."

"Because I knew it would be disastrous for your career," he cried. "Of course I wanted you to come out. Do you think it was easy being with someone I couldn't talk about? Or someone I couldn't stand next to at the podium after you won the Super Bowl?"

"You hate football! Lane, what the fuck? You never ever expressed any interest in my job when we were together. I even asked you if you wanted to come with me to some of the team parties, remember? I told you I'd be happy to introduce you to the team as my partner if you wanted. I specifically remember you saying you had no interest in being around a room full of 'dumb jock homophobes.' Those were your exact words."

His chin came out in defiance. "And was I wrong?"

I rubbed my hands over my face. "Yes! The team and the League have been amazing."

Lane's anger seemed to evaporate. "I don't want to give up on twenty years of history, Christian."

I reached out and took his hand, speaking as gently as I could. "I don't want to lose you in my life, Lane. But we're not meant to be together like that. If we were, I would have come out years ago and you would have stayed. Even when we were together and things were good, you always had your eye on other people, other places. And at the time, I figured that was the price I paid for not being able to go all in. But now I realize it was because I wasn't enough for you. I'm your safe place, Lanie. In this small town, it was so much easier for us to come back to each other than try and find someone new."

Lane looked toward the side of the house where Hayworth was. "I don't want you to be with anyone else."

I let out a laugh. "That's not the same thing as you saying you're in love with me and want to be with me."

A smile began at the corner of his mouth. "You're cute and all, but..." He winked. "Just kidding. You know I love you."

"I do." Silence landed between us. "Do you want to meet Hayworth?" I asked.

"Fuck no. I'm not that mature. Not yet, anyway. Sorry."

"I completely understand. I'd probably feel the same way if I saw you with someone in town."

"Really?"

"Lane, we were together on and off for two decades."

"Maybe we could get together and catch up a little? I mean, as friends?"

"Absolutely. I'd like that."

He pulled his lip between his teeth and stood up. "I'd better get going. I'm sorry for interrupting your... ah..."

I followed him to the front door. "It's fine. He's here for a week, but maybe after that we can meet for lunch?"

Lane threw himself into my arms and held on tightly. I felt the familiarity of his body, but for the first time it didn't feel comforting the way it always had before. It was a little too short and a little too... not Hayworth.

"Be safe heading back to town," I said, releasing him.

When I closed the door behind him, I turned to see Hayworth standing in the doorway to the kitchen.

"I think I should go," he said.

## 17

———————

## HAYWORTH

WHEN WE'D ENTERED the house, I'd gone immediately into the small study and shut the door, not even stopping in the open kitchen long enough to fix the coffee I'd wanted. I didn't want to hear Christian be kind to his ex. And I knew he would be because he was a sweet man. But I wasn't. I was the kind of man who was sick and fucking tired of competing with everyone's childhood sweetheart.

I pulled out my phone and called my sister, Bailey.

"Is it important? I'm in the middle of a *Great British Bake Off* marathon," she said over a mouthful of some kind of snack.

"Press pause, I'm having a crisis."

"Shit," she mumbled. After a few muffled movement noises, she came back. "Spill. Wait, aren't you in Wyoming?"

"Yeah." I felt my throat thicken and begged myself not to get emotional. "He... he has this ex-boyfriend, and... um..." I swallowed. If I started crying, I was hanging up the phone and throwing myself out the nearest window.

"Hay," she said softly. "Is the ex there at the house?"

"Mm-hm, yeah."

"Take a deep breath, brother. Where are they right now?"

"Talking in the other room."

"Did Christian ask you to leave?"

"No."

"Did he act... I don't know, weird around you in front of his ex? Like he didn't want the guy to know you were together?"

"No. He didn't let go of my hand. And then he kissed me on the cheek."

Bailey sighed. "Hay, you're overreacting. That's not how a guilty guy acts. He wouldn't have done that if he wanted to get back with his ex."

My sister was naive and stupid sometimes. "Not true. He would have if he was trying to make the guy jealous."

"Oh, Hay." She sounded sad, and for a brief moment, I thought she finally got it and was commiserating with me about the loss of this fine man. "You're such a fucking idiot."

"What? Jesus. Way to kick a guy when he's down, Bailey."

God, I hated sisters.

"You think just because Beau picked Maverick, Noah picked Luke, and Josh picked Cyrus, that means you're never getting picked. But that's bullshit. Those were different situations, Hay. All three of those guys had been hung up on those men since they were teens. They picked their childhood sweetheart over you. That's not the same thing as going back to any old ex-boyfriend."

I stared at the dark fireplace that had been so warm and inviting during my last visit.

"Lane is his childhood sweetheart, you asshole," I said numbly.

"Oh, shit," she said.

"Yeah."

"Hay, that doesn't mean—"

"Save it," I said. "I gotta go."

"Wait! Hay!"

I hung up on her and turned off my phone, standing up and heading toward the door. I couldn't do this anymore. I couldn't pretend someone like Christian Lasley would want someone like me long term.

When I made it to the doorway of the kitchen, I saw them by the front door.

Christian was smiling at Lane. "It's fine. He's here for a week, but maybe after that we can meet for lunch?"

Then they were in each other's arms, and I felt like maybe I wasn't even going to make it to the front door before bursting into tears like a baby. It was a confirmation of my greatest fear.

My feet froze where I stood, and I couldn't move.

As soon as he closed the door behind Lane and turned toward me, I blurted, "I think I should go."

Christian's face fell. "Why? Because Lane was here?"

"No, it's fine." *It's not fine.* "I don't mind." *I do; I mind so damned much.* "I'm fine." *Like hell I am.* "I can just go." *I can't feel my face or move my feet.*

Christian approached me cautiously, reaching out and cupping my face when he got close. "You're pale," he murmured. "And you're trembling."

"I'm fine," I repeated stupidly. How many times was I going to use that stupid word? I smiled at him and his eyes widened. "Really. I'm… it's okay."

"It's not okay. Clearly, it's not okay. You're shaking." He put his arm around me and steered me back to the small den where he sat me in a chair and knelt to start the fire.

I buried my face in my hands and tried to calm down. How could I explain to him that I understood—that what he had with Lane trumped whatever it was the two of us were doing?

# 18

## CHRISTIAN

"Talk to me," I urged, kneeling in front of his chair and taking his hands into mine. "Are you upset because of Lane?"

"You've been amazing," Hayworth began. And it sounded like the next word out of his mouth was going to be "but."

"Hay..." I said, hoping to stop him. "Please don't..."

He seemed to realize what I was thinking. Suddenly he was in my lap with his long arms around my neck and his face in my neck. My arms came around him and squeezed tightly as I rocked back against the base of the other chair.

"Talk to me," I begged. "Whatever it is, I'll fix it."

"It's not that." He pulled back and met my eyes. "You're not going to pick me in the long term. And then you're going to regret the time lost with him. I think... I think maybe you should invite Lane back to work things out."

I stared at him while his words scrambled to find purchase in my brain. "What in the hell are you talking about?"

"The two of you have history. You've been together forever. He's your childhood sweetheart."

"So? He's not the one I'm with. I'm with *you*. At least, I think?"

Hayworth rolled his eyes. "We both know the two of you are going to end up together. That's how these things work. So I'd feel bad for him if down the road he was still confronted with the time you dated some random guy and had all these photos in the press."

I couldn't believe my ears. I held him away from me by his shoulders. "What the *fuck* are you saying right now?"

As I stared at him, I suddenly realized Hayworth looked miserable. He even seemed to be on the verge of tears.

I immediately pulled him back in my lap. "Hay, baby. Tell me what you're saying. Do you not want to be with me?" I reached out and cupped his face. The slight trembling I felt in his body was familiar now. He was scared.

"I do, of course I do. It's my fucking dream. But I know it's not going to happen. It's okay, Chris," he said in a broken voice. "I know he's important to you. I just think something like this—the pictures in the media—should be with the person you're going to end up with. Not someone short term."

"Why isn't it going to happen—you and me together?"

He couldn't make eye contact with me. "I'm not the guy that gets picked. I'm the guy you have the rebound relationship with. Everyone I've ever dated or wanted to be with has left me for their childhood crush. It's just... it's just how it is. And I think maybe part of it is because I'm not relationship material, you know? Some guys aren't."

I was stunned. He'd told me about a couple of guys he'd wanted something more serious with in the past. Both men had ended up with their childhood love. Surely he didn't think that had anything to do with him? The thought made me want to scream.

"Hayworth Buchanan," I growled, leaning down and grabbing his chin to force him to look at me. "At the risk of scaring you off, I am falling in love with you. Not temporary lust. Not rebound bullshit. Love. The kind that makes me want to turn my game room into a recording booth and clean out half my closet for your preppy buttondowns. Hear me right now. I am not in love with Lane Young. I never felt for him the way I already feel for you. I do not want to share my life with him or even have my picture taken with him. I want to do those things with *you*."

His eyes filled while I spoke until one of them overflowed.

"Baby," I said softly, thumbing the tears away. "God, please tell me you believe me. And that you think maybe someday you'll feel the same about me."

He nodded, tipping out more tears. His hands came up to dash them away, but I grabbed his wrists to stop him. "I already do! Fuck," he muttered. "This is stupid. I'm sorry. God, I'm acting like a baby."

I leaned in and kissed up the trail of his spilled tears, tasting the salt on my tongue. "*My* baby," I murmured between kisses. "And feeling insecure about someone like me who is obviously a bad bet is understandable. I'm just sorry I didn't realize that's what was happening. I would have reassured you sooner."

"No, you did. You've been super sweet. I'm being immature and stupid. I'm so fucking embarrassed."

I kept kissing his face, which eventually seemed to help him relax into me.

"Chris, you must think I'm so needy. God."

I pulled back and met his eye. "You are the least needy person I've met. At every single stage of this, you've stopped to make sure I'm okay. You asked if I wanted to stop the interview. Then you asked if I was sure I was ready for you to air the podcast. You offered to stay out of sight of the media at the Raider stadium, and again at the hotel. You fucking offered to step aside for my ex to come back. There hasn't been a single time you've put yourself first, Hayworth."

"You're more important," he said. As if it was a fact.

"Bullshit. *You*. You're more important." I settled back against the chair and rubbed my hands up and down his back. "Hay, sweetheart. I want you to be happy. What will make you happy?'

"You. This. Being here makes me really happy."

"Me too," I said, leaning in to kiss him gently. We kissed slowly for a little while before I thought of something. "Will you let me tell you about my conversation with Lane?"

**19**

———————

HAYWORTH

I FELT SO stupid and needy. How in the hell could a man as put together as Christian Lasley want to be with someone so childish and insecure? I wasn't proud of my little breakdown; I was mortified.

I blew out a breath and smiled at him. "No, you don't need to tell me anything. What's between you and Lane is none of my business."

"Not true. If you and I are starting a relationship—and I hope we are—then you deserve to know that my relationship with Lane is completely over. When I arranged to meet him for lunch, it was our agreed-upon effort to just be friends."

"You have so much history together," I said. "Are you sure you—"

He stopped me with a thumb over my lips before stroking it along my jaw, making me shiver. "That's why we decided to try and be friends. Having history together doesn't mean you should stay together as lovers. In our case, the back-and-forth was the pure path of least resistance. It was easier to go back to each other than find someone better."

I leaned my head against his shoulder and snuggled into him so I didn't have to see the look in his eyes when he answered my question. His arms were solid and strong around me. "Does he want you back?"

"Not really. I think it's a case of not wanting anyone else to have me either."

His hands felt warm on my back as they moved up and down over my shirt. "I know how he feels," I muttered.

Christian laughed and tipped my chin up to drop a kiss to my lips. "I think if I met your old friend Beau, I might feel homicidal. So I can't imagine how it felt for you to see Lane here."

"It felt like I wanted to sic my new pony on him," I admitted. "Or… or something."

"Can we talk about the difference between a pony and a foal please?" he asked with another laugh. "Because it's starting to become a problem. If you're going to date a rancher, you kind of need to know."

"No. Because it's been approximately 168 hours since I last saw you naked, and that's unacceptable." I stood up and held my hand out to him, but he didn't move. Christian looked at me with laser focus.

"Take off your clothes, Hayworth."

I looked around, catching a glimpse of the kitchen through the open door and the snowy field outside through the study windows.

"What, here?"

"Here."

My dick stiffened in my pants. "But—"

"Now. Get naked now."

I began unbuttoning my shirt. "Am I doing this solo?"

"Do you by any chance have a condom and lube in your pocket?"

My dick got even harder. "No. But there's some in my bag in the car."

"Stay here. I have some upstairs. When I get back, I want you naked on the floor in front of the fire. Do you understand, Hayworth?"

Jesus fuck. Bossy coach was sexy coach.

"Uh-huh," I breathed.

He pinned me with that stare for another beat before he got up slowly and sauntered out of the room as if there was no hurry whatsoever.

It took him approximately 168 more hours to get back with the supplies. By then I was stroking my cock and leaking all over my stomach. As soon as Chris saw me, he moaned.

"Fuck, Hay," he groaned, pressing a hand against his cock.

"Bring that here. Are you going to fuck me this time?" I'd gotten the feeling he was in the mood to top, and I was happy as hell to bottom for him. "Please?"

"That okay?"

"More than. C'mere." I reached out and began tugging at his jeans as if they'd come down that easily. Christian laughed and quickly stripped before kneeling down to lie on top of me. His body felt so damned good—warm and solid, cock hard and hot—I wanted my hands everywhere.

Chris peered down at me and time seemed to slow. His hands came up to bracket my face. Before he could open his mouth, I chucked a bunch of words into a blender and flicked it on high.

"I love you. I do. Oh, god. I hope that's... yeah. Well, yeah. I do. So... there's that. And—"

Thankfully, Christian took mercy on me and interrupted my word smoothie with a kiss. Then he smiled down at me with patience and adoration.

"I love you too, baby. So much. And I want to prove it to you over and over until you really do believe it."

"Want to feel you inside me, Chris," I whispered. "Want you as close as possible."

We kissed for what felt like hours until finally neither one of us could wait any longer. Chris took his time spreading lube around and inside my hole before putting on the condom.

When he finally pushed his cock into me, I gasped and pulled him closer, chanting and begging and groaning until even that had been replaced by gasps and sighs and the slapping of our bodies together.

Our eyes locked together until each of us found our release, clutching onto each other and shouting each other's names.

It was the first time in my life I finally understood what people meant when they said there was a distinction between having sex and making love.

And I finally learned the reason none of my previous relationships had worked out.

This was exactly where I was meant to be. And Christian Lasley was who I'd always been meant to love.

"Love you so much, Hayworth," he murmured beneath my jaw where he dropped tiny kisses. "Want you to say here forever. With me."

I hadn't told him yet about my interview with ESPN. About how they'd offered me a regular segment on their show and had even agreed to allow me to broadcast from anywhere in the country. I pictured the two of us working together to turn one of the rooms in the house into a dedicated recording studio the way he'd envisioned. I imagined spring days in the off-season spent learning to ride horses and winter nights during playoffs watching games together in front of the fire unless the Jackals were playing, in which case I imagined cheering him on from the stands until I was hoarse from screaming.

But more than anything else, I looked forward to sharing my life with a man who deserved to be adored and who seemed quite willing to let me love him the way I always wanted to love someone of my very own.

"You okay, baby?" he asked, leaning up on an elbow to peer down at me.

I nodded and drew a finger along his collarbone. "So beyond okay. I'm happier than I've ever been. I love you."

His face was soft with affection and tenderness, so his words surprised me and made me laugh. "Do you love me enough to let me explain why Buck isn't a pony now?"

Instead of answering, I reached up and tackled him, rolling him onto his back and kissing him until both of us were hard again and ready to go.

It was going to be an amazing week. And I wasn't about to let it stop there.

# EPILOGUE
## CHRISTIAN

*Two Years Later*

I LOOKED up at the handsome man on the stage in the classic black tuxedo with the red hearts bow tie. Seeing Hayworth relaxed and smiling behind the podium never got old. As insecure as he sometimes was in real life, on stage, Hayworth was a natural.

"The SNN award for Best Male Olympian goes to..." He looked inside the envelope. "Oh sweet! Happy Valentine's Day indeed... the winner is Gus Kenworthy! Be still my beating heart."

The crowd went wild, both for Gus, who deserved it after his stunning performance in Beijing, and Hayworth, who'd become a fan favorite at ESPN since his segment had earned incredible ratings. The network had recently offered him a massive promotion and salary bump if he'd relocate to their headquarters in Connecticut. I'd offered to look into a position with the Jets or Bills so we could move for his job, but he'd finally confessed to being too happy at the ranch to want to move.

When he'd turned down the promotion, the network had agreed to let him have it if we agreed to upgrade his studio. He already had contractors planning on meeting us for bids when we got back from this awards show gig. Not only had he been chosen to present some of the awards, but I'd been nominated for one.

After another award presentation, Hayworth snuck back into the seat next to mine and leaned over for a quick peck on the lips.

I grasped his hand in mine. "Good job, babe," I whispered.

"Did you see Gus kiss me?" he teased. "I think we're dating now."

"He kissed you on the cheek, and we're scrubbing that thing with pumice when we get home."

His eyes crinkled from laughter before he looked forward again to watch Shaun White announce the best jockey. Hay leaned over to whisper again, his breath warm against my neck.

"You think he knows what a jockey is?"

"Hush," I chastised, squeezing his hand. "You're one to talk."

"Hey, I ride horses."

I thought of his near death riding Buck the week before. "Baby," I said, trying again to hold in a laugh. "I think it's more that horses ride *you*."

"They're not the only ones."

After a few more awards and the accompanying cheering and clapping, it was finally time for the Best Coach award. Serena Williams stood at the podium to announce the nominees.

"If they don't pick you, I'll give you a pity blow job," Hay whispered. I felt my face heat and wondered if the cameras were on me.

We'd been to two other awards ceremonies together, and I finally realized this was how he kept me smiling for the cameras. He leaned over again and spoke from the side of his mouth.

"Would this be a bad time to tell you I'm pregnant?"

I bit my tongue to keep from laughing out loud.

"I swear I was on the pill. But I think my boyfriend poked a hole in the—"

"And the winner is... Christian Lasley of the Jackson Jackals! Coach Lasley is known for winning the Heisman while at Nebraska, catching the winning Super Bowl pass while playing for the Denver Broncos, and bringing home three additional Super Bowl wins as a coach for the Jackson Jackals, including this year's championship just two weeks ago. In his personal life, Coach Lasley is known for raising beef cattle in his spare time on his ranch in Wyoming as well as recently marrying popular sports comedian Hayworth Buchanan of ESPN's Hay Sports. Coach Lasley, come on up here."

I turned and kissed Hay on the lips, holding him under the chin for a few extra beats before pulling back and mouthing *I love you*.

He said it back to me before slapping me on the ass and telling me to go get my award.

When I stood at the podium looking out at the sea of athletes, coaches, journalists, and fans, I thought about how lucky I was to have found someone to share it all with.

"Thank you so much. I'd like to thank my team and the League, without whom none of this would be possible. My parents for raising me to work hard and go after what I wanted. And most of all, the love of my life, Hayworth Buchanan, for standing by me every step of the way and loving this game as much as I do. Now if you could just stop featuring all my screwups on your show each week, that'd be great..."

The audience hooted and cheered, most likely thinking back to the episode of Hay Sports in which Hay had spent a solid half hour riffing on the Jackals' game against Houston. It was the now-infamous game during the regular season where I'd gotten so pissed off at one of my players for causing a horse-collar penalty, I'd lunged toward him and been horse-collared by my own headset. Hay had laughed for days about that.

And of course, the podcast had gone viral.

I winked at him from the podium and laughed when he buried his face in his hands. When I walked backstage, he was there. Someone had retrieved him and brought him back there to congratulate me. I thought about the champagne and chocolate waiting for us back at the hotel and the special late dinner I'd arranged for the two of us in the room. After the craziness of a fantastic season culminating in the Super Bowl victory, I was ready to spend some time focused solely on loving my husband and showing him why he was my favorite human on earth. What better time to do it than Valentine's Day?

I hugged him long and hard. "You're my favorite teammate ever. You know that, right?" I asked.

He nodded into my neck. "And you're my favorite coach."

*Thank you for reading! Want more Hayworth? Check out* Moving Maverick *in the Made Marian series, where he was originally introduced. Hay also appears in* A Very Marian Christmas *and the short story "Josh" which can be found in* Made Marian Shorts. *Turn the page for more information on Lucy Lennox, including how to find other free stories.*

*Up next is* Made Marian Mixtape, *book nine in the Made Marian series! Made Marian Mixtape presents over ten new stories set in the Made Marian world that will make you sniffle, swoon, and laugh out loud.*

*Want more Marians? Grab* Facing West *to begin the spin-off series featuring the Marian cousins!*

# THE MARIAN FAMILY

**Thomas** and **Rebecca Marian**

*Their children (oldest to youngest):*
**Pete**, married to **Ginger**
**Jamie** (meets **Teddy** in *Taming Teddy*)
**Blue** (meets **Tristan** in *Borrowing Blue*)
**Thad** (dating Tristan's cousin **Sarah**)
**Jude** (meets **Derek** in *Jumping Jude*)
**Simone** (dating **Joel Healy**)
**Maverick** (meets **Beau** in *Moving Maverick*)
**Griff** (meets **Sam** in *Grounding Griffin*)
**Dante** (meets **AJ** in *Delivering Dante*)
**Ammon** (gets rescued in *Delivering Dante*)

**Aunt Tilly** - Thomas Marian's aunt

**Non-Marians**

**Granny** - Tristan's grandmother
**Irene** - Granny's wife

**Harold Cannon** - Tilly's boyfriend (first appears in *Delivering Dante*)
**Noah** (appears with **Luke** in *A Very Marian Christmas*)
**Ben** - Griff's biological brother (meets **Reese** in *Made Mine*)
**Gideon** - Ammon's biological brother (meets Hunter in "Let It Snow",
*Made Marian Mixtape*)

# LETTER FROM LUCY

Dear Reader,

Thank you so much for reading Hay, a short in the Made Marian series!

If you haven't tried my Forever Wilde series, check out *Facing West*, which is the story of Griffin Marian's best friend Nico.

Be sure to follow me on your favorite retailer site to be notified of new releases, and look for me on Facebook for sneak peeks of upcoming stories. You can also join me on Patreon for exclusive content and behind the scenes glimpses.

Please take a moment to write a review of *Hay*. Reviews can make all the difference in helping a book show up in searches.

Feel free to sign up for my newsletter, stop by www.LucyLennox.com or visit me on social media to stay in touch. To see fun inspiration photos for all of my novels, visit my Pinterest boards.

Happy reading!
Lucy

# ALSO BY LUCY LENNOX

Find me online → https://linktr.ee/LucyLennox

Read my books:

Made Marian Series

Forever Wilde Series

Aster Valley Series

The Billionaire Brotherhood Series

After Oscar Series (with Molly Maddox)

Twist of Fate Series (with Sloane Kennedy)

Licking Thicket Series (with May Archer)

Champion Security Series (with May Archer)

Honeybridge Series (with May Archer)

Find a complete list of my stand alone romances and novellas at www.LucyLennox.com along with audio samples, freebies, suggested reading order, and more!

# ABOUT LUCY LENNOX

Lucy Lennox is the USA Today bestselling author of over fifty gay romance titles including the GoodReads Hall of Fame winner Wilde Love. Born and raised in the southeast USA, she is finally putting good use to that English Lit degree she earned before the turn of the century.

Lucy enjoys naps, pizza, and procrastinating. She stays up way too late each night reading romance because it's simply the best.

For more information and to stay updated about future releases, sales and audio news and to grab some free and bonus reads, please sign up for Lucy's author newsletter on her website at LucyLennox.com or to stay in the know, join her exciting reader group, Lucy's Lair on Facebook.

facebook.com/lucylennoxmm

instagram.com/lucylennoxmm

amazon.com/Lucy-Lennox/e/B01N0IOYPT

bookbub.com/authors/lucy-lennox

patreon.com/lucylennox

pinterest.com/lucy_lennox